Blackbird

and 11 other dark stories

Anson Hunter

Copyright © 2021 Anson Hunter

Blackbird

All rights reserved.

ISBN: 978-1-8381887-6-4
anson.hunter@hotmail.com

DEDICATION

This book is dedicated to everyone that reads, enjoys and then re-tells any of the stories.

ABOUT THE AUTHOR

Anson Hunter is the pseudonym of Tom Boniface-Webb, who is the author of several books on music, including 'I Was Britpopped' and the 'Modern Music Masters' series.

CONTENTS

Please note, some of these stories contain graphic content that might not be suitable for all readers, including sexual violence, and I'm very sorry to say, a dead dog.

BLACKBIRD

Section 1 (<u>The Killing Moon</u>):

Before I met her, I used to fall in love with a different girl every day on the tube. She put a stop to that. After that day, this day, this girl on this day, I get the feeling I won't be falling in love with another girl tomorrow.

Christ, she's so beautiful…

Is this stalking? Surely not. I'm just walking along a London street. I'm allowed to walk along a London street, aren't I? It's not a private street, I can go anywhere I like, can't I? Except I have no idea where I am, or where I'm going. Plus, it's just me and her. The irregular clip-clop of her high heels on the cobbled back street the only sound.

I look up, new moon, new beginnings. Is this the start of something new? An incipient allegory for a new life.

It was her smell that hooked me first. Quite the typical day by any other standards. At this very moment I should be sat on my sofa with half a bottle of Bells and a tired TV dinner, but I'm not, instead I'm here.

On the tube – buried in 'Nuremberg: Evil on Trial' – I would have missed her had we not been suddenly forced together when the train jolted. An initially belligerent hand on my chest knocked the breath from my lungs but was immediately juxtaposed by the face full of the sweet smell of heaven's own nectar, and then a mumbled apology and blissful stomach-churning smile.

And that was that.

What am I hoping to achieve? Surely the moment of talking is long past. This is now just someone following someone else. This is stalking.

I stop, turn to face the wall and light a cigarette, needing time to think. The white cloud of smoke billows off into the ether, heading toward the new moon. The clip-clop sound disappears off into the middle distance and I watch as she turns a corner down another, darker alley, taking with her all my clichéd hopes and dreams.

I turn to leave, realising how ridiculous I've been, when I catch the sound of something. What was it? Surely nothing. Or was it…a muffled cry for help? Could be. Plus, there's no longer that clip-clop sound.

I make it into the alley just as the dark receding figure hurries round the corner at the other end. She's sprawled on the ground. I'm at her side in seconds.

'Are you ok?'

She's shaken but not hurt. He'd grabbed her bag but then run off when he heard me coming.

'You saved me,' she purrs, grateful eyes and a breaking smile. 'You saved me…'

I help her up and catch sight again of the new moon hanging resplendent in the sky behind her. The Killing Moon.

Christ, she's so beautiful…

Section 2 (<u>Blackbird</u>):

A full moon.

I can see it through the French windows, hanging over the river and peeking between translucent grey clouds, like in a cheap b-movie horror film from the fifties.

She enters and re-fills my glass with whisky, grinning with red stained teeth and sucking down more Shiraz.

'I know,' she coos, crossing the room and abandoning her glass momentarily on the table, swaying slightly as she selects a CD and places it clumsily in the tray. No-one else could get away with being so clumsy. No-one else could make it look so attractive. She pulls off her jumper and drops it unnoticed on the floor, where it will stay until I put it in the dirty-linen basket.

'*Blackbird singing in the dead of night…*' she coos along with McCartney, somewhere between tuneful and tuneless.

Perhaps more toward tuneless. But it doesn't matter. No-one else could make tuneless sound so attractive.

'You're my blackbird.' She points a finger as she sways in time with the music. Is it in time? 'You swooped in and saved me in the dead of night…'

Christ, she's so beautiful…

'*Blaaack-biird… flyyy…,*' she continues, procuring her glass from the table and knocking the reminder of its contents back in one go. A stray splat of crimson liquid hits my cream woollen carpet.

'Sod it!'

She's on all fours making it worse with her hand.

'Don't worry about it,' I hear myself say, across the room at her side within seconds, stopping her hand with my own. 'It's fine, don't worry…'

She stops and sits back on her haunches, laughing absurdly.

'I love you,' she lies, leaning forward and flinging her arms round my neck and kissing me deeply. The taste of cheap Shiraz fills my mouth.

'I love you too,' I reply.

Only one of us means it.

Section 3 (<u>Just Like Honey</u>):

Another full moon.

Christ, has it been a whole month already? A whole month since I found out. I feel numb, but that could just be the cold. The buildings lean over me, mockingly, so I light yet another cigarette, more out of the need for something to do rather than actual want. I don't think I'll ever want anything ever again. Just one thing.

Somewhere up in the building that I'm stood in front of a girl is breaking my heart.

Comfortable amongst the orange glow that separates this flat from the other darkened deadened ones the girl I love is writhing in pleasure that I could never offer her with a man that's twice the man that I am. I know this because I've seen them together. I've followed them together. I followed them here tonight, and I'll wait outside until she leaves and follow her home. With him there was none of the casual clumsiness, she was too self-conscious, too aware of trying to impress. None of that with me.

It's poetic justice in a way. A relationship that started as a lie must end as one too. But is this really the end? A relationship ends when one of the two parties doesn't want it to go on anymore. Is that true? But what if the other party doesn't want it to end? What happens then? Does it continue? Even if just in the mind of the wronged party?

I reach for my half empty half bottle of Bells and sink back a healthy slug. That'll keep the cold out. Amongst other things.

Finally, she leaves.

I've been stood still so long and have smoked so many cigarettes that I'm not sure I'm able to walk. But I manage. Of course, I do.

Christ, she's so beautiful…

She heads off down the road as the rising sun twitches at the corners of the light grey London sky, that irregular clip-clop of her high-heels again the only sound. It's a replica of that time. But so much has happened, so much has changed. I've changed. Has she?

Aware of being watched I look up at the orange window and catch sight of a voluminous silhouette looking down, watching her, watching me, watching me watching him, and her. Hands in pockets I head after her, through the iridescent puddles.

If only this was that first time. Nerves mixed with adrenaline at what I was doing. The peculiar feeling of anticipation at stepping outside of myself, of following my gut, of living out a long latent fantasy. And of succeeding. Chance, luck and fate finally conspiring in my favour and giving me what I wanted, what it felt like I needed.

What a fool. Just like Romeo, fortune's fool. Except Juliet loved Romeo.

A shrill buzz cuts through the air. Her mobile. She answers it quickly with a deft 'hey' and then mumbles something inaudible. She half glances over her shoulder.

'… yeah, I know…' I hear her hiss.

He's told her. He's warned her. And she doesn't care.

I remember the scent of her perfume that first time. The scent which is so intrinsically linked with her. That scent that grabbed me, reached deep inside me and planted a malignant seed that wouldn't let me go, that had now become so much a part of me I could never imagine or want a life without it. That smell, that succulent, tender tenacious taste. Just like nectar, just like honey.

She can't take that away from me.

Just let her try.

Section 4 (<u>Polly</u>):

My hand hurts. My knuckles sting. That's her fault. I wriggle my fingers and wince against the shot of pain emanating from my middle knuckle. Could be broken. That's her fault. Kurt Cobain grunts away in the background. Polly wants a cracker.

She smiles. Is it a smile? Could be a grimace.

'Drink?' She ignores me. Bitch! Can't even answer a simple question. It's not a smile or a grimace, it's a grin, a sarcastic grin. I feel a swell of rage rising from just where that malignant seed was planted, right in the centre of my being. I swing out, feeling a resultant reduction in tension after contact.

I pour another whisky, noting my shaking hand, and press the glass against her lips. She flinches and lets out a sound, like a yelp. Not quite a yelp, but like a yelp.

'Drink!' I say, tilting the glass so that the coarse brown

liquid pours some down her chin, some into her mouth, then finally some down her throat. The yelp is replaced by a gulp, then a cough, then a lolling of the head. 'Drink,' I repeat. 'It'll help. Trust me.'

Eventually she lifts her head, it seems a real effort, resistant strands of feathery dark blonde hair stick to her face. She looks me in the eye. There is something saddened there. Something that looks like it might have died.

Finally, she understands.
She tries to say something, and red spit covers her chin. I can't make it out.

'What was that?' I ask, leaning in close and cupping my hand round my ear. I'm now so close I can smell her. It gets to me. Something tweaks deep inside and I feel my rage shallow. How does she still smell so good? Even in this state. Only she could carry off looking and smelling so good in a situation like this.

Christ, she's so beautiful…even through broken teeth and past blood-stained features…I look outside and catch sight of the new moon. New moon, new beginnings.

I lift my whisky glass to my lips and drain it dry.

MORT

It's amazing how closely the blood seeping across the living room rug resembles red wine. A thick full-bodied Merlot perhaps, or an Argentinian Malbec. Despite the dark, opaque colour, the deep burgundy is prominent on the cream wool, mirroring the similarly coloured Rothko print that hangs on the living room wall. What was the name of that Cabernet Sauvignon you liked from Bordeaux? Was it this dark?

After about five minutes the rug is close to saturation. Totally ruined now, I suppose. Where had we bought it again, Harrods? How much had it cost? A month's wages, apparently. Whatever that had been.

In all though, I think you would have been happy with the aesthetics of the scene. I'm glad you wore your white shirt. Most of the blood drains forward from your head wound onto the rug, but a splash cascades contrarily down the back of your shirt, like a Jackson Pollack. You see, I learned something you taught me about art.

All that talk of red wine has made me fancy a glass, and I wander idly over to your wine cabinet, the thrill of touching what I'm not allowed triggering a surge of excitement to course through me. The realisation that you are no longer around is slowly beginning to filter through. It's an erotic excitement and I feel my cock stiffen. My breath shortening. Slowly, I unzip my jeans and the excitement swells. I couldn't. Could I? I turn back to face you. You don't seem to object. The wine will have to wait, for now.

Afterwards I carefully select a bottle that you would never have let me anywhere near and place it on the coffee table. That coffee table. A wedding present from your aunty and uncle something-or-other. I never met them. Suppose I never will now. They live in Japan I think, or I might just be thinking that because of the tawdry far

Eastern design on the table. I had never wanted it anyway. It was hideous. It had been your choice, and now it is going to go.

The rug would have to go too. It's a shame, but the once beautiful colouring – egg-shell white, if I remember correctly – was now close to black. I guess if I had pre-planned this whole escapade, I could have moved it first. But it wasn't planned, and now I had to live with the consequences. One of which is getting rid of the beautiful egg-white rug that I think had come from Peter Jones.

It's unlikely that anyone will come knocking tonight, so I sit down on the sofa, looking down at your defunct body, splayed in its final position. The final position you'll ever take. If it had been planned, you probably would have opted not to have your left arm drooped over your shoulder, leading down your back not unlike one of my yoga positions, but I'm afraid you didn't have the choice.

Is your finger pointing? 'Look at this,' it seems to suggest. 'Look at all this blood, my shirt is ruined!'

I can't help the mirthless chuckle that escapes my mouth. It's the first noise that has sounded in the space since your final grunt, and the suddenness of it shocks me. Some music perhaps. Nina Simone. You had good taste in music. I hadn't liked her when we had first met. More of a Whitney and Mariah boy, but just like everything else in my life you had drilled her into me, and now I couldn't imagine listening to anything else. I place the wine glass on the coffee table that I have now decided to get rid of and cross the room toward the record player. My record player. Nina it is.

It's strange. Now that it's happened it feels like there was a strange inevitability to this outcome. How old had I been when we met? Twenty-three, maybe just twenty-four. Still a boy, really. You had been forty. I remember that clearly. I had been working behind the bar at your fortieth birthday party. We had shared a snog in the toilets. You were so drunk, I had thought it just one of those things that straight guys did and then pretended it had never happened. But you had left your girlfriend to be with me. Eventually. After lying to her for three months. That hadn't felt very good. She seemed like the dependable sort. A kind, passionless woman, happy to sit somewhere in the background. She drank vodka and slimline tonic with fresh lime. You can tell a lot about a person from what they drink. Hers showed her to be dependable. Boring. Square, you would say years later when you finally could. Square, but dependable. I wonder what she might be doing now. Re-married? Probably no kids. Too old. I wonder if she will come to your funeral. I wonder if we'll have a funeral. I could wear white, you'd hate that kind of show-offish-ness.

You had even come out to your parents a year or so after that. Grudgingly. Something I had never expected. Your father hadn't taken it well. Not because he was homophobic, he said, he was all for gay rights, but not as far as allowing us to marry. That was one step toward equality too far. He had been in the army, you said, no-one questioned what went on behind closed doors in the army, but that didn't mean that they wanted it shoved down their throats.

No, rather, he didn't take it well, because he said he didn't believe you. And now, looking back all these years later, I think I finally understand what he meant. You hadn't really sounded very convincing. I'm not sure if you really meant it yourself. It was more like reluctant acceptance, like how one might accept being diabetic, or short-sighted. A crux, rather than a way of life to be celebrated. He had sensed this and had clung to it. If you didn't accept it, then he didn't need to either. And your mother just went along with what her lord and master decreed.

He had fallen ill in early 2013 and had died a few weeks before same-sex marriage was legalised in 2014. Not the long, drawn-out death that you had anticipated. Still short enough to be considered a shock. His death had made you more determined to marry and we had been one of the first hundred or so couples up the aisle at Marylebone Town Hall Registry Office, your weeping mother – the ink on your father's death certificate still wet – and my discombobulated parents, our only guests. Why hadn't we invited our friends? Shame? We had thought we were caught up in the joyous bubble of love and the romance of a quick marriage, but now I wonder if you weren't ashamed of everyone seeing us. Perhaps I was being paranoid. You certainly told me I was. You threw a lavish party for us, that was true, it was quite the night. Why hadn't we had it at home? I wanted to show off our lovely South-Kensington flat, but apparently that hadn't been possible.

I had expected things to be easier once your father had died, and we were finally free to live our lives the way that we wanted to, but if anything, you grew more and more into yourself. Your opinions drifted slowly away from the liberal to fall more in line with the right-wing conservative rhetoric that your father spouted after too much wine at the dinner table. In his absence you began to adopt his persona and slowly fill the void that he had left behind. I had never realised how much he had meant to you. Was that why you denied your feelings for so long? When we had met, I had felt privileged to be the person to finally help you transition toward your true nature, but I wonder now if I was merely the final straw that broke the camel's back. It was bound to happen whether you wanted it to or not, and now that it had, now that you had given in to the base level urges, and now that there was no-one there in the shape of your father to reprimand you, you would have to take on that character yourself. You would have to become your father.

Not long after that, in fact, just a few days after we

returned from the hedonistic idyll that had been our Saint Tropez honeymoon, was the first time that I could no longer ignore the monster that was slowly taking over you. I wonder now whether you had let yourself go with such wild abandon in the South of France because you felt it was the last time that you would allow yourself to. And because you were so far removed from what you would call your life.

You had hit the drink and drugs like you were wishing there was no tomorrow and had even suggested a threesome with the virile young Turkish boy we had met. I had thought you were joking. We were on our honeymoon. You had told me you were joking. But I later considered that you probably meant it. You were trying to exorcise something from your system which wouldn't leave. The more you tried to push it away, the deeper it seemed to burrow into you, and the more frustrated you became. You were trying to deny your nature in a world that no longer needed you to.

The first time you hit me was under the most trivial of circumstances. Spilt coffee beans on the cool white kitchen counter surface. 'Who cares,' I had said, trying to make light of it. 'I fucking care!' had been your gritted teeth response. I had laughed. We had always laughed about such frivolous things. 'Leave it for Magda,' I had said, dismissively. You had left the room and I had thought no more about it until you returned a few moments later and smacked me so hard round the back of the head that it made my ears ring. I was stunned. You left immediately and disappeared into your study. The suddenness and brutality of the act made me wonder whether it was someone else that had smacked me. Not you, but an imposter, a darker, more menacing version of you. Or, that it hadn't happened at all. That I had just imagined it. At bedtime you said and did nothing out of the ordinary. So I said and did nothing either. I never told anyone. I was ashamed. It was so out of character for you, and I told myself that it was a one off. Marriage is hard, you have to work at it. People make mistakes. You move on and grow together.

But you did do it again. That first time had knocked down some invisible wall and each subsequent transgression seemed much easier. Then it just hung there like a threat in the air whenever there was a disagreement between us. And each time it happened, it was that much harder for me to tell anyone.

'Why didn't you tell someone sooner?' I heard people ask, unable to consider that their usually headstrong friend could put himself in such a position. So, I pulled away from my friends too. An act that you actively encouraged. We only needed each other, you would often say. Then I heard you answer my mobile, telling whomever it was that I didn't want to meet up, and that if they didn't hear from me not to hassle as my life was moving in another direction anyway. Why didn't I say anything then? Was I still telling myself that I wanted the marriage to work? Was I now trapped in a disastrous union of my own making? The door was always open. I could have walked out at any time I saw fit. Why didn't I?

You fired Magda, and after I lost my job at the bar because of continual absence, you suggested I just stay at home. You made more than enough to support us both, so why not? Then for my next birthday, you bought me an apron and a mop. It was a joke, you said, but the implication was obvious.

I had no idea about our finances. If I ever wanted any money then I just had to ask, but the only things I ever seemed to buy were groceries and cleaning products. You were secretive about how much you earned, which must have been a lot because the things that you bought were expensive. The flat must have been expensive. The rug, the wine, the paintings. I was never told how much anything cost but took on the role of dutiful housewife with as much of the dignity as I could muster.

When we had married, I had taken on your name. Davies. So bland and ordinary. But it was always going to be me that took on your name. Obviously. And that simple act seemed to shed me of my own identity entirely. You even insisted on calling me the gender-neutral Jo. Not Joe. But Jo. I saw you write it down more than once. Mortimer and Jo Davies. It wasn't a husband that you wanted. It wasn't a partner that you wanted. You realised that you had no power over your nature and who you were attracted to, but you could control who you were with, and as it turned out, that was all you needed.

You even encouraged me to grow my hair long. To shave myself all over. It's cleaner, you said. If it was so much cleaner, why didn't you do it yourself?

That night. This night. The night that things finally reached their zenith we had gone to bed as soon as we had arrived home. It was late, and you had to be at work early, but you were horny, and so we had fallen onto the firm, expensive mattress pawing at each other, tearing off clothes, not unlike we had when we had first got together. Initially I might even have called it romantic, if its occurrence hadn't been so noticeable due to its infrequency. You pushed me onto my back, threw my trousers dramatically across the room, and entered me with one solid, uncomfortable thrust. Then you grabbed my cock, which was the only time that you seemed to acknowledge its existence and hung on to it whilst you came with the virility I hadn't seen for years.

That evening we had been at your boss' house. Usually you would have gone alone, but he had insisted on partners joining and I had stood in a small group of wives and girlfriends, expected to make small talk whilst the real men discussed much more important issues. It wasn't that I wanted to be treated like one of the big boys, stood with you, laughing about high finance, but neither did I want to be treated like the woman that you would have preferred me to be. I had nothing against the wives, but I wasn't one of them. I'm not a woman, I'm a man. There is another way.

They were all nice enough, and your colleagues all smiled and treated me warmly, it was only you that seemed uncomfortable to have me there. At dinner you had spent the whole time faced away from me, talking to someone else's partner, and after we had eaten you had disappeared out onto the balcony. Your boss had asked me how I was feeling. I told him I was fine, to which he seemed slightly confused. Apparently, you had told them I was suffering from ME so unable to leave the house much. I wondered why you let the lie drop for tonight, surely knowing that your deception would be revealed. Perhaps you simply didn't care any longer.

Spent, you had stood and padded out of the bedroom in your socks, doing up your trousers as you went. I lay on my back, your cum dribbling out of me, my wilting cock laying discarded on my stomach, and thought what a sorry sight I must have looked. I wonder now, still sat on your sofa sipping your red wine, whether that moment was my final straw. Without thinking too much about it, I stood and located my own pants and left the bedroom after you.

Out in the living room you were stood with your back to me, stretching after the exertion, just like a jungle cat having finished a particularly satisfying feed. You must have heard me enter the room but hadn't turned. You were done with me. Just like the wilting cock that you only liked to think about when you wanted sex, I was now forgotten.

The statuette was situated on the mantelpiece to my left. All I had to do was reach out and pick it up. Who was it a likeness of again? I wondered whether it was Eros, the Greek god of erotic love, how fitting that would have been, but I don't think it was. The figure was of a man with a bull's head. A minotaur.

Without thinking, I reached out and picked it up, feeling the satisfying weight in my hand. Still not thinking, but feeling the requisite adrenaline begin to flood my system, I stepped forward, the statuette raised high, my head joyously empty. I would worry about the ramifications later. Would it be best to cut your body up before disposing of it? Would burying be better or burning? What were your online passwords? What about the pre-nup you'd got me to sign? I would figure them all out later. For now, I knew what I needed to do, and that task was the only thing that mattered. Goodbye Mort. Goodbye forever.

LIFE BY THE SWORD

'C U NEXT TUESDAY x,' reads the text message, with no hint of its own irony.

'Not if I see you first…' someone with a voice that sounds a bit like mine croaks back.

Sleep now a defunct possibility, I drag my legs languidly over the side of the bed and pull myself awkwardly to an upright position, attempting to check my gyrating head at the same time. How much had I drunk? Fuck knows. What time is it? Fuck knows…later than it should be.

At this point the events of the previous night sometimes filtered back to me in a disjointed erratic fashion, certain movements, sensations or even smells could trigger a multitude of alcohol enacted and then dulled memories rather forgotten than recalled.

But not this morning. Thank fuck.

The en suite is only a few feet away but seems such a struggle to reach. My swollen feet are like sacks of wet cement slovenly crawling their unabated way across the boarded floor. Eventually I collapse onto the toilet and piss for what feels like an hour, wondering idly what the hell I had got up to the night before.

When done I knock back a pint of beautiful water from the bathroom sink and then feeling that familiar tingling in the back of my mouth throw the lot back up again in one clear motion, it's mixed with what could once have been a chicken kebab. Done, I catch sight of my naked form in the bathroom mirror. Fat. That is the only word I can think of. Fat and hung-over.

When was the last time I hadn't thrown up like that first thing in the morning?

The tube is busy, but I force my way into the middle of the aisle and gratefully collapse onto a seat after a few stops, ignoring the glare of an old lady stood nearby. She moves over as if to say something, but she seems to change her mind as I slip my coat off. Sorry lady, my need is greater than yours today. As I drift off into a semi-sleep some of the events of the night before filter back to my cloudy comatose mind.

'You are one fucked up kid!' yelled the c u next Tuesday girl, as we knocked back tequila shots at some anonymous neon coloured bar.

She could only have been a year of two older than me.

When I reach college, the refectory is much more appealing than the tutorial I was about to miss for the fourth week. I squeeze myself onto a stool at the bar and order a pint of cider to take the edge off, gaining a few looks from the scattered students. My watch tells me it's just gone 10.30am. God bless early opening. Just one or two here and then to the library.

And that's where she finds me an hour or so later. I don't look up. I don't need to, that shuffle across the worn carpet is unmistakeable.

'Thought you were going to come and see me last night?' she says.

'Yeah, sorry. Got, caught up in something. How was class?'

'Fine. How much have you drunk?'

'That much,' I lie, pointing to the three quarters full pint in front of me and cursing the damn student staff for not yet clearing away the other two empties, hopefully she won't notice.

There is a brief pause in which my immediate fate and chances of getting some that evening are internally debated and then she shuffles off the way she'd come.

Fuck.

I catch up with her outside and grab her arm, twisting her round to face me.

'Why don't you come inside and we can sit down, have

something to eat.'

'I can't, Alex,' she whines, avoiding eye contact. 'I've got my antenatal class.'

Something makes me reach out and place my hand on her protruding belly. How many weeks was she now, twenty-four? … no, twenty-five.

'Why don't you come?'

'Why should I? It's not mine.'

'That's not what I meant… I…'

She trails off and I take my hand away from her belly and light a cigarette, blowing the smoke away from her as best I can, then waving my hand in her face when the wind blows it back.

'I wish I could do that,' she says.

'No-one's stopping you.'

She shakes her head and makes to push past me, but I stay her with a hand on each shoulder, the cigarette drops to the ground.

'Let me go.'

I lean in and kiss her clumsily on the mouth, forcing my tongue past her gritted teeth until I feel her own on mine. She relents after a further moment or two and then I feel her breathing deepen and soon she kisses me back, unable to stop herself.

Eventually I pull away and she smiles despite herself, all forgiven. I run a hand through the dark blonde hair she has held up in a loose ponytail, seemingly the only way pregnant girls can have their hair. Her face is flushed but it suits her. I want to tell her that I love her, but can't quite find the words, and then the moment's gone.

'You sure you don't want to come?' she says, kissing me again on the mouth, this time lingering and letting her tongue slip past my lips first.

In way of an answer, I step back, giving her the room to pass me. She sighs and makes to push past, turning with an afterthought.

'Meet me after?'

I nod, lighting another cigarette.

'And Alex, please, nothing more to drink.'

'No choice,' I say, holding up my hands. 'No money left.'

She sighs again and I watch her waddle away wondering whether I would meet her after, knowing I probably would.

My phone buzzes and I pull it out of my pocket.

'I'm waiting in the reception,' it tells me.

He was waiting for me outside the school office. A crumbling grey man of about fifty with hunched shoulders and a too tight brown rain mac.

'Alright, dad,' I say as I approach him, catching the stare of the young receptionist and glaring.

'Alex, how are you?' he asks, turning to face me and affixing a grin, his lawyer's grin. He probably thinks it isn't the same, but it is.

'Fine.'

'Great… great. And the course? Going well?' He gestures at gormless Denise behind the reception desk as if she embodied the ideal student. How ironic.

'Yes, fine.'

'No tutorial this morning?'

I shrug and we both stare awkwardly at the floor for a moment or two. Then he steps forward and places his right hand purposefully on my protruding belly. Just like I had done to her moments before. I flinch, but don't move away.

'And how is… the little one?'

'Yes, fine.'

'Hope you're looking after her. Have you… heard anything from the father?'

I think back to who the father could be. Any one of a number of poor sods: Rob, Brian, Ian, Titch… probably not Titch. None of them are half the person she is. I wished I had gone with her to that antenatal class after all, the place we'd met just those few weeks before, bored eyes meeting across an otherwise coupled room.

'Listen, I was thinking. Perhaps you would like to come and live with me. For the last few months. I could… help.'

Over my dead body.

'I dunno, dad. I think I'm kinda doing alright.'

'It's only going to get harder you know.'

'I've got support,' I lie. I hope. She is due two weeks before me. Would she stick to the pact and hang around, or would she buckle and return to her folks? No-one would blame her if she did. I wouldn't blame her.

I watch his shoulders visibly sag. He is running out of steam, the fixed grin slipping. Over his shoulder my phantom mother eggs him on, jabbing him in the ribs in that malicious way of hers, telling him not to give up. But he can no longer hear her.

'Well at least let me give you some money then.'

'Ok.'

'Have you thought about any names?'

'What was mum's name?'

He knows I know full well and I see the question form on his lips before he lets it slide away.

'Margaret,' he says, again looking away, knowing what I am going to say before I do.

'Then at least we can count one name out.'

And that's that. He's gone. Full of kisses and cuddles and promises of calls and further visits. I head back to the refectory to wait for her, the money he had not yet transferred already burning a hole in my pocket.

LA NASCITA DI VENERE (THE BIRTH OF VENUS)

Venus was glum. That was the only way to put it. Life wasn't quite panning out how she expected it to. Life wasn't quite panning out how she had been assured that it was her divine right to. She swirled the last of her vodka and coke, took a tiny sip and coughed lightly to cover the lull in conversation.

It wasn't easy being the most beautiful woman in the world. A fact that those who weren't would do well to remember, thank you very much. Let them try it for a day. If nothing else, it meant that she was near irresistible to almost every male. And most of the females, for that matter. She glanced over at the bar to where Kevin was procuring another round of drinks and spotted at least a dozen young men staring back at her, not even pretending that they weren't, trying desperately to make eye-contact. Why on earth had they come to such a trendy busy downtown bar? She usually would have steered well clear. This type of thing always happened with the guys that frequented such places. Thank Jupiter they weren't in a sport's bar again. That evening had been an unmitigated disaster.

Her glace to the bar had caught the attention of all the wrong egos, and already she could see friend turning against friend as masculine pride swelled and testosterone surged. She'd have to leave soon. One of them would sooner or later pluck up the courage to come over and that would be that. Luckily, she had the excuse that her father wanted to see her. Who could argue with that?

So as not to incite the lustful masses further, Venus turned back to her two companions at the table and forced a weak smile. As a unit they forced one back but didn't offer any placatory conversation. They were the reason that the group was drinking in this bar, it had been their idea and they had done it for the simple fact that they hated her. In many ways they and their type – namely, women – were worse than the blokes. The bitchy back-handed compliments and passive aggressive attacks of jealously at Venus' beauty and sexual allure were often just too much for her to bare. And they all wanted to have sex with her too. They rarely admitted it… actually that wasn't true… Shaz, who was now fingering the last slither of ice in her otherwise empty glass, had tried it on numerous times over the last few years, but was now quietly seething across the table, struggling with the conflicting clash of disdain and sexual allure. They hated themselves for being attracted to her, and as such took it out on her. They were worse than the blokes. At least the men's anger was usually only ever directed at rivals for her affections.

Neither was she totally comfortable in the company of the gays. Jupiter!, she'd made that mistake before. Base-level naivety that there was straight and gay, and no middle ground, had led her one sad time into letting her guard down whilst hanging out with a seemingly innocent young gay chap, only to find him bursting in on her whilst she was having a wee in the pub toilets, and declaring his undying love for her. Luckily, Kevin was different.

'Drinkies, ladies…'

Kevin's arrival immediately lightened the weighty mood and Venus felt herself relax, the refreshing of the drinks (if only momentarily) even reversed the disdainful looks of Shaz and Liz.

'Alright there grumpy-chops? Penny for them.'

She couldn't help but smile at Kevin's chubby little innocent face. She had no idea what she'd do if she didn't have him. He was, in fact, one of the only two people she could name that weren't uncontrollably sexually attracted to her. The other one was her husband.

It had been her father, Jupiter, King of the gods, who had firstly suggested, then insisted, and finally forced Venus into such a ridiculously unsuited partnership. And mostly, she suspected, because she had rejected his advances.

She smiled at Kevin's question, but didn't immediately answer, and he soon became distracted by the conversation that Shaz and Liz had fallen into, so as not to look like they were seething at Venus, whilst still seething at Venus. She tried to look on the bright side. Things could be worse. She was after all a goddess, so, eternally youthful and immortal to boot. Plus, she always got a good parking spot, and could eat pretty much anything that she wanted without getting fat. Except all she every wanted to eat was ambrosia and nectar. She had often thought that getting fat would be a blessing, at least then everyone she looked at wouldn't look back at her envisaging what her head would look like knocking against their headboard.

It wasn't even as if she could really focus on work. Professionally she had been incredibly unsuccessful. She hadn't paid that much attention at school, and as such was trained for nothing. She hadn't had to try at school because as soon as she'd grown tits at the age of twelve she had predictably found herself receiving A's for every subject without having to ever turn in a paper.

The short spell she'd had as a model had also proved a total disaster. Which really was an incredible shame because on paper it really should have been a fairly obvious vocation for the goddess of love. The photographer of her very first photo session had lost first his reputation, then his job and finally his sanity after refusing to hand over the proofs from the shoot. She really did feel that the fates were conspiring against her sometimes (namely because they each fancied her, despite their blindness). And then of course there was the other small problem. Well, actually there were two small problems.

In fact, that wasn't true. There was one problem that was small in physical stature but big in figurative relevance. Then there was another problem that was neither small in physical stature, nor in figurative relevance. The first was the seed now growing in her belly. The second was the man who was not her husband who had put it there. She was incredibly fertile, that was another rather annoying thing. No nine-month gestation period for her. He had only fucked her three days ago and already she was beginning to show. She took a long slurp of her vodka. At least she could drink during pregnancy. There was no danger of the baby being harmed. Oh no, that child would be perfectly fucked up all on its own.

Clearly noting her unease, Kevin looped his arm through hers as he chatted amicably with Shaz and Liz about nothing in particular. He glanced over at her and on catching her eye, winked. Thank Jupiter for Kevin. Totally and utterly gay and as such neither attracted to Venus, nor resentful of her power over others, 'The only female things I've put my willy inside,' he'd told her once, 'were my mum's knickers when I was about seven, and was trying something out.'

She was about to speak, at least attempt to join in the inane conversation, when her eye-line was drawn as someone approached the table. It was one of the buffoons who had been hovering around the bar, and this was presumably their spokesman. The most dominant one come to try his luck with the goddess of love. He was going to regret it.

'Excuse me,' he bleated, his voice shaking as any of the alcohol-fuelled bravado drained from him once he was stood directly in front of her.

Venus affixed a half-smile, ignoring the glares from across the table. 'Yes?' she purred gently. She was careful to only half-smile, having learnt the hard way the effect a full beamer could have on he who it was directed at. Every member of her school year with a surname beginning with a letter later in the alphabet than hers probably still held it against her for what had happened to Headmaster Fitzwilliam. Apparently he'd recovered remarkably well, but was no longer allowed near children.

'I… I…,' stammered the young man, his features growing a darker and darker shade of scarlet. Venus could make out his friends at the bar, not even bothering to stifle the laughs at how he was faring.

'It's ok,' said Venus, after the poor chap had failed to move his sentence beyond 'I…', 'it's not your fault. Why don't you go back over to your friends?'

The broken fellow turned on cue and slunk back over to the bar, following Venus' orders, to where his friends were only too eager to begin their mocking.

'Morons,' grumped either Shaz or Liz, but Venus hadn't stopped staring after the young man, who was being ridiculed by his so-called mates. Being a victim of it herself, she hated bullying.

'You should have told the lecherous git where to go,' added either Liz or Shaz.

The boy at the bar looked as if he were about to cry, and Venus could take it no longer, and so with a graceful flourish she near leapt from the table and glided across the floor space to face the pack of buffoons.

They stopped mocking as one and all stared as she stood to her full (and yet still rather tiny) height in front of them all. Hands authoritatively – yet still really quite sexily – on hips.

'Yes?' she began, speaking to a sea of faces just like the first chap's. 'Got something to say?'

Silence.

'No? Nothing witty or cutting from the safety of the bar? No? Dickless wonders.'

And with that she turned and sashayed back over to the table, collapsing daintily onto her seat, grabbing her drink and draining most of it back in one.

'Nice one babes,' said Kevin, taking her hand in his, 'but you've got'ta be careful, that was dangerous.'

No, it wasn't. It was anything but dangerous. Venus was fully aware of the effect she had on pretty much every man, apart from Kevin (and Vulcan). It was fairly similar to the effect that one man had on her.

Mars was a soldier, meaning that he was away for months on end, fighting some distant foe somewhere distant, and often bringing back with him many unwanted exotic presents. Venus had thanked Jupiter many times that gods and goddesses couldn't contract venereal diseases or Jupiter only knew what state she'd be in.

It was hard to say exactly what it was that she was attracted to. The simple answer would have been his deep confidant brooding, his raw sexual magnetism, and his huge pectoral muscles (not to mention his enormous cock), but all of that was easily counter-acted by the sheer size and scope of his ego and level of unadulterated arrogance. The man was a total dick. Perhaps they were just meant for each other, destined to be together in some ancient written – can never be undone – sort of way, like her father and stepmother. They had first acted on it when they were teenagers, and Jupiter had caught them at it in the pantry at the annual feast of the gods. He had married her off to poor old Vulcan pretty much straight away after the feast. That didn't stop Mars though. The fact she was married. In fact, if anything, it spurred him on more, and meant that he didn't have to worry about marrying her himself. He was usually back a day or so, but soon enough and without fail, he would turn up at her door, stinking of ale, and with his huge bear like grip he would pick her up and whisk her off to the nearest bedroom, or sofa, or armchair, or work surface, and she was power-less to resist. And whether Vulcan was in the room or not.

Poor old Vulcan. He hadn't wanted much out of life, and he certainly hadn't wanted her. He was quite contended to hobble around in his workshop, banging and crashing and creating subtle masterpieces of engineering genius that no-one but he seemed that fussed about. His reaction on their wedding night had been enough for him. All she'd done was take her top off and he'd fainted. Then when he'd come round, he'd locked himself in the en suite and refused to come out until the morning. A few days later he'd instructed Mercury to castrate him with a huge pair of metal work tongs, figuring that if he was going to be married to Venus, he couldn't go through that every day. As solutions went, it was quite an affective one, and there now existed a domestic harmony of sorts between husband and wife, much better than either of them might have anticipated. He just had to make sure to go out on the nights that Mars came around. Which at the moment was likely to be fairly often.

On cue, her phone beeped and she extracted it from her bag. It was from him, of course.

#meet at yours in hour#

Ever the lothario.

She text back:

#can't, gotta see dad#

A few moments later he responded.

#what about?#

To which she replied:

#dunno#

#I'll cum too#

#ok#

Just what she needed, her father and her lover in the same room.

Despite being on top of a mountain some way outside of the city centre, Venus found herself stood outside her father's house just under an hour later. It is pretty easy getting around when you're a god, but despite that, she still used her car, leaving the little pink MG in her designated parking spot not far from the great banqueting hall. Jupiter's house should perhaps more accurately be described as an enormous mansion, comprised of many different and not always complementary styles, depending on what took his fancy at that particular moment. Venus crossed the threshold, the gigantic entrance not dissimilar to that of the Taj Mahal, and soon found herself stood in the main hallway, which was modelled on the Whispering Gallery of St. Paul's Cathedral in London, complete with the several hundred-foot drop to the stone floor far below. Venus had no idea what was down there, and had no intention of finding out.

'Ahh, there you are my dear. Do come through.'

For the king of the gods, Jupiter was really quite tiny – when she wore heels, he made even Venus seem tall – but it was the quietness of his voice that most noticed first. Venus thought it had something to do with the fact that everyone had to listen to him – being king of the gods – so why talk loudly. He stood far away on the other side, and had he not spoken, she may well have not noticed he was there at all.

Venus sighed and circumnavigated around the gallery, following him as he retreated into the room beyond. She knew immediately what was up. It was the same thing every bloody month, but she followed none the less, knowing she'd have to go through the motions. The décor of Jupiter's lounge had changed dramatically since her last visit, and now would not have looked out of place in the house of a seventies porn baron. He collapsed onto a beige velour chaise-lounge, winked and patted the seat beside him. Venus didn't move.

'Where's Juno?' she said, crossing her arms.

'Mummy's not here,' replied Jupiter, suggestively, wiggling his eyebrows up and down. 'Whilst the cat's away…' He lifted his hand up and made a cat's claw, swiping in Venus' direction. Venus smiled weakly.

Jupiter was a notorious womaniser, but not one who garnered success through any kind of charisma or subtlety, but rather women slept with him because as king of the gods they had little choice but to. If power was a great aphrodisiac, then Jupiter's oily demeanour worked incredibly well to balance this out. Young ladies found they often had to go to great odds to avoid his advances, one young lady locked herself in her family basement and another in a huge wooden trunk that ended up in the sea.

Jupiter was not to be dismayed though, and he just began to create more and more elaborate means of seduction, including disguising himself. Poor old Leda thought she was being petted by an overly excited swan only to have the damn thing hump her silly by the riverside when she was going for a walk; and Danaë, the daughter of a king none the less, found herself being seduced by a shower of golden light as she listened to music lying on her bed. Poor girl had no idea what had happened until she found herself carrying a demi-god a few days later. Not easy to explain that one away to your parents, 'honestly dad, it was this warm golden glow, I promise...'

Jupiter patted the seat next to him once more and just as Venus was considering crossing the room toward him – mostly to make sure he stopped the cat clawing – the door was flung open and in burst the huge ball of sinew and machismo that was Mars.

'What the Pluto is going on here?!' he screamed, crossing the room in two long strides and grabbing his father by the lapels, lifting him off the sofa and high into the air.

'Take your hands off me you great buffoon!' screamed Jupiter, incandescent with rage. Mars, now in such close proximity, realised what he had done and followed his father's instructions, releasing him and letting him fall flat on his face on the floor far below.

'Oh shit,' he said, fleeing back across the room, past Venus and nearly out of the door.

'Stop right there.'

His voice was quiet, but Mars froze in his spot, hanging his head like the scolded child that he was. It wasn't that Jupiter did much actual governing, that was left to the humans, but you didn't get to be king of the gods without commanding respect from those around you, notably the ones that you had fathered.

'Turn and face me, boy.'

Mars, his chin still touching his massive chest, gingerly turned around to face the music.

'Hi, dad,' he said. Venus stifled a giggle, perhaps it was the familiarity of the scene, but she couldn't help thinking that if it wasn't so pathetic, this little drama would be hilarious.

'Apologise to me and your sister and then we'll talk about your punishment.'

'S-sorry dad, s-sorry Venus.'

'Fucksake,' said Venus, rolling her eyes.

Sometime later Venus stood on the bridge next to the river Styx. The river separated what everyone referred to as 'the real world' from the underworld and unless you were a god or dead you couldn't go any further. She was thinking about the events of the day, and her existence in general, and wondering what her next move should be. All in all, it hadn't been a great day, in fact she felt worse off than when it started. If she'd stayed in bed all day, then she would have been in a better position than she now was. Maybe that's what she should do tomorrow.

Her father had tried yet again to seduce her. Her brother had tried to beat their father up and had been banished to some far-off distant war as punishment, and now she was going to have to raise their child alone. Not that he would have been much use in that respect anyway.

She took her phone out from her bag and dialled the only person who she knew would make her feel better.

'Hello?' he said.

'Hi Kev, it's me, can you talk?'

'Er… no, not now babes… soz… I'll bell you up later. Bye.'

He hung up and Venus was left looking at the small piece of plastic in her hand. On an impulse she chucked the phone into the river below and watched it sink out of sight.

'Fuck 'em,' she said out loud to no-one in particular, and wandered back toward town. All in all, it hadn't been the best of days, but then, there was always tomorrow.

DINNER PARTY

The Isle of Dogs can be so eerily quiet at night-time, particularly at this time of year. The snow seemed to exaggerate this, amplifying even the tiniest of noises, whilst the dark added an air of sinister mystery to the otherwise usually concordant surroundings. The only sound was the stifled crunch of mine and Derek's boots on the off-white three or four inches of snow, as we trudged our way to the all-night shop. With each passed corner suspense rose then fell as the expected group of belligerent gang members failed to leap out at us. Once or twice I checked over my shoulder just to make sure they definitely weren't there. Not in the five years that I'd lived in the area had I encountered such a group, but there had always been something about the dark and the quiet that unnerved me, and there was a first time for everything.

'Hope it's still open,' I said, suddenly self-conscious of the silence hanging between us.

'What do you think Jude meant with that comment about my paunch?' whined Derek, who had clearly been pondering on my wife's mention of his expanding waistline at dinner.

'Paunch? She said, 'seasonal spread'. I think it was supposed to be endearing.'

'Well, it bloody well wasn't. Seasonal-bloody-spread. What does that even mean? It's Christmas time. S'posed to put on a few pounds at Christmas, aren't you? Keeps the cold out, putting a couple of sodding pounds on.'

He sucked hard on the last of his Marlboro Light before flicking the butt onto the ground ahead of us, where it stuck in the snow with the tip facing upwards. Instead of being extinguished it seemed to relish in the support and continued billowing its plume of smoke into the still, frosty air. I wondered if we would see it on our return journey.

'Bloody cold,' Derek added, shoving his hands deep into his coat pockets, and thus ending that chapter of our conversation.

Ravi's was open. Ravi's was always open. No matter what day it was, what time it was or what the weather conditions were like, Ravi's would always be open for overpriced beer, vile wine and cheap frozen pizzas. In the summer he even got rid of the door, it just got in the way, apparently.

We loaded up half a dozen mixed bottles of red and white, two bottles of Smirnoff and a dozen cans of Heineken for Derek on the counter – I never touched the stuff – and added sixty Marlboros. Ravi, never really one for conversation, buzzed the lot through and took my credit card without making eye contact.

'Busy night?' I asked, to which he responded with half a sarcastic smile. It hadn't been then. 'Well, it's the snow isn't it,' I added to no response at all. So I turned to Derek and in way of conversation said, 'Soph was on her high horse a bit earlier, wasn't she?' Derek shrugged and grabbed the larger two of the bags, in part being helpful, but in my mind exerting his own superior level of masculinity over me. He often did this in front of girls, tiny unnoticeable things to anyone but me, a jab on the arm that was just that bit too hard, or an arm round the shoulders that on appearance seemed affectionate but would increase in pressure until I was forced to double over in an increasingly uncomfortable headlock. He had perhaps grown so used to doing it now that he either felt like he needed to do it in front of the oblivious shopkeeper, or it had just become a subconscious reflex action.

I had always thought it balanced itself out with my much-advanced intellect, and when we were at university this might have been the case, but in the subsequent ten or fifteen years it had become less and less so. We had always liked to argue, and once I had been able to wind him up so much that he would become iridescent with rage, resorting to violence, leaving me in bouts of pain, but firmly on the moral high ground. This hadn't happened for years. Was this a sign of his developing level of maturity over the advancing years, or the improvement and evolution of his argument?

'She can get like that after a couple, you know that,' he said, pushing the seasonal door open with his foot and heading back out into the cold. I grabbed the lighter two of the bags and followed.

The high horse I had been referring to had occurred at dinner and had been part of the reason Derek and I had used the excuse of escaping to the shop for a few minutes solace. The discussion – as always – was on politics, which none of us knew or cared enough about to have a proper opinion on, until we were drunk and in each other's company, when we suddenly knew everything there was to know and more. This would inevitably segue into the other hot and banned-from-dinner-parties topic of religion, which in this instance I actually did know a little bit about, teaching as I did at an inner-city secondary school where some thirty languages were spoken and something like five hundred gods worshipped by the thousand or so students. I had in fact been just about to bring this up and wrestle the moral compass back in my direction and away from Derek, whose job as some-kind-or-other banker made any points he iterated on the subject immediately redundant and indefensible, when Soph chirped up with, 'No-one cares anymore anyway. If they actually talked about things that people cared about then they might pay more attention.'

This was typical of Soph. If she ever felt like the conversation was moving away from her, or the attention hadn't been placed squarely on her for more than a few minutes she would steer it back toward something that she could talk about, and then back it up with some banal example from her own life. Such as: 'If it was more like X-factor, where each candidate was on a Saturday night show and they had musical accompaniments, and you could phone in, then more people would vote. Me and my friends would anyway…'

Jude and I didn't even need to make eye contact. We had discussed this trait of Soph's character so often that the mere pause of the wineglass she was lifting to her lips – that I caught only in my peripheral vision – was enough to make us both giggle, Jude tactfully hiding hers behind a cough and subsequent gulp of her wine. Derek noticed, as he always did, but said nothing. Soph herself sensed a slight shift in the atmosphere and self-consciously pushed a strand of her dark blonde hair behind her ear – an extremely cute and girlish gesture – before sipping from her wine.

I had often suspected that she was nowhere near as stupid as she often made out, but played up to the part as we all tended to do in such situations. Comfortable and familiar with the way our relationships had developed over the years, we acted our parts without even thinking about them, becoming perhaps completely different people to those that we were with our other friends or work colleagues. Soph was the dumb blonde one, Jude was the athletic feminist one, Derek the sporty city banker one, and I the studious thoughtful one. Whether we were actually these characters or not was now irrelevant, as too much water had passed under the bridge for us to be anyone other than the people that we were when we were with each other. I wondered what would happen should one of us end up with a different partner.

'Well, the proof of the pudding is in the eating,' Soph persevered with. 'More people voted in the X-factor final than in the last general election. That says it all really.'

'There were more *votes* in the X-factor final than in the last general election,' corrected

Jude, maintaining her Poker face admirably.

'That's what I said.'

'No. You said more *people* voted. That's not true.'

'Same difference.'

'Well, no it's not. You can only vote once in a general election. You can vote as many times as you like in X-factor.'

'We know what you meant, darling,' added Derek in a benevolent attempt to placate his wife.

To say my feelings toward Soph were confused was something of an understatement. I had always wanted to sleep with her, that was for sure, but I had always managed to delude myself that what I really needed to turn me on was to be stimulated mentally as well as physically, like I was with Jude. This was of course total nonsense, and was finally proven to me one year when we had holidayed together in the South of France. I had bustled into their room in the villa, late for a game of golf with Derek, to find him going down on her. She was on her back on the bed, facing toward me totally naked, her large natural breasts heaving as she breathed heavily and evenly, clasping the back of Derek's head, fully in control as she moved him up and down to her own contentment, a beautifully relaxed and serene look covering her face. I froze, swore and then turned as quickly as I could and ran straight to the outdoor toilets, not even registering the mixed smell of urine and faeces until I had masturbated in record time.

Afterwards I tried to analyse what exactly had turned me on so much. Perhaps it had been the shear fact of catching them at it, but the more I thought on the subject there had been something in her demeanour, she had been so relaxed and so in charge, she knew what she wanted and she was going to get it. There was none of the silly dolly-bird image that she gave across at social situations. If you get her in the right context she seemed to totally lose control whilst remaining totally in charge at the same time.

Perhaps this was what Derek saw in her, and why he constantly placated her. Was this another one he had on me?

I was somewhat disappointed to see that Derek's cigarette was no longer burning as we trudged our laden way back along the street, it was instead replaced by a small black hole in the snow where an inch or two of grey pavement was now visible, the sodden butt sat in the midst of it.

We walked in silence, the only sound that vaguely reassuring crunch of boot on snow, combined with the congenial tinkle of the glass bottles building anticipation for our return. When we were twenty or so feet from the metal gates that separated my flat block from the rest of London, Derek squinted into the evening gloom.

'What's that on the ground? Was that there when we left?'

At first it appeared to be a discarded pile of rags, but as we drew closer it became apparent that a person, a young girl, was lying in the snow. On closer inspection she was unconscious but breathing, a light cloud of breath streaming from her bloodied mouth.

'Looks like she's been beaten up,' I said, putting down my bags and kneeling beside her in the snow. All I could see was her face but that appeared bad enough. Her nose was bruised with both nostrils visibly blocked with dried dark brown blood. Her lip was split and the much more rouge and prominent blood that still seeped from it covered most of her chin and neck.

'She's probably been mugged,' said Derek, still stood some feet away. A shiver arched through my body at this suggestion, and I felt a sudden need to be inside my cosy flat. 'What should we do?'

'Call an ambulance, would probably be the best bet. Help me get her inside.' I stood and put a hand under each armpit, expecting Derek to grab her by the feet, but he didn't move. 'Give us a hand will you,' I added impatiently.

'Are you sure we should? What if it's a trick? Like a Trojan horse or something. She might wait 'til we're all asleep and then let all her mates in to do God knows what.'

'It's not a sodding Trojan horse, Derek. Look at the state of her. We can't leave her here.

Let's get her inside and then we can call an ambulance, and the Police.'

At the suggestion of the Police his ear pricked up. 'Police?' he asked, actually taking a step back into the road.

'Yes, Derek. The Police. As you so caringly pointed out yourself, she's clearly been mugged.'

Reluctantly Derek leant down and picked up her feet, and unwilling to let go of the carrier bags we started the long struggle of getting the poor girl inside, complete with clinking bags and all.

Once through the door Derek's reluctance to call the Police became immediately apparent. The girls were doing coke. And suddenly all became clear. I hadn't been a huge fan of cocaine for some years, I felt like it made me paranoid and to put it quite frankly: a bit of a dick (as it does everyone), but Jude would have been up for it, so knowing that I was likely to cause a bit of a fuss, she would have convinced Soph, who had subsequently convinced Derek, not to start until I was out of the house and so by my return it would be too late to object, and if I then did it wouldn't matter anyway as they would already be coked up so wouldn't care.

As the front door slammed shut behind us Jude bandied round the corner, her bottom jaw rotating like an upside-down helicopter – she was so obvious on coke – ready to welcome our return, until she saw the unconscious girl, we were carrying between us and stopped so quickly Soph, who was hurrying along behind, collided into her.

'Who the fuck is this girl?' asked my darling wife.

'Forty-five-fucking-minutes!' she yelled after I was off the phone to the Police. 'What the hell are we supposed to do with her until then?'

'It's the time of year. They're busy, it's snowing. Besides, it'll give you plenty of time to hide your narcotics, won't it.'

'Sod off!'

'And you wonder why I don't like you on coke.'

'Get over it, Hermione, this isn't bible camp, I can do what I sodding well like in my own home!' I thought about saying, 'It's my home actually,' as I had inherited it not her, but then realised we'd probably get into the whole marriage and sharing debate as we always did, which she would inevitably end with her favourite line, 'Well maybe I'll divorce you and we'll see who's house it is then.' Instead, I made a shushing sound, which I knew would irritate her, and said, 'Can you keep your voice down please, we've got company if you hadn't forgotten.'

Derek and Soph had dragged the still comatose girl into the spare room and to avoid Jude's come-back I pushed the door open to see how they were getting on. Jude followed me into the room, not wanting to be left out. They had taken the girl's coat off and laid her flat on the bed. Soph sat gently stroking her greasy black hair, whilst Derek stood staring at the girl, looking awkward.

'Jude,' I said over my shoulder. 'Could you get a flannel and some bandages please. Least we could do would be to clean her up a bit.'

Jude opened her mouth as if to reply, but thankfully realised what a churlish action it would be to argue, so rather moronically turned – mouth still open – and headed back out of the room and down the hall.

Usually my wife was a thoughtful and reserved woman, without a malicious bone in her body, a trait which I had discovered made a girl very easy to fall in love with. Men in their twenties want wild and exciting girls, but as they grow older and more accustomed to their creature comforts the opposite becomes true. Despite the odd bit of path-straying back into the wild territory, a man ultimately wants a woman who will look after him. Someone had once told me that you slept with the whore but married your mother. Well, Jude even had the same shoe-size as my mother. This was not to say that she was at all vapid or without passion (not that my mother was…), she was extremely opinionated and fun loving; she just cared about her family and her future, and so put her priorities in careful order. In essence there was not really anything wrong with her, she seemed to have everything in the right place, and it was this that made the whole thing so much harder. If there was just one thing about her that wasn't perfect for me, it would make it all so much easier, because as I grew older I discovered more and more things about myself that I was not happy with, and so things seemed unfairly out of balance. I supposed I was worried that she would one day notice.

It was very likely that I put her on a pedestal, I'm sure there were a hundred things her friends and family couldn't stand about her, but for me there wasn't really anything substantial, whereas with myself there were a hundred things that she hated. I seemed to irritate her constantly, sometimes on purpose to get a reaction, but mostly through no real fault of my own, which often left me with a sense of unguarded vulnerable inadequacy. It also meant that as much as it annoyed me, I relished nights like tonight where I could finally look down at her, shaking my head knowingly when she acted in an immature fashion, knowing that – gratefully – these nights were few and far between.

She returned a few minutes later, her coke high having at least abated for the moment, and the two girls set about cleaning the poor young waif from the worst of her injuries. Derek and I – confirming to the obvious sexual clichés – used this as an excuse to retire to the living room, where I quickly procured the bottle of Glenfiddich Jude's father had given me for Christmas and sat heavily on the sofa with it and the crystal cut whisky glass which Jude's sister had given me for Christmas, grateful for the moment of peace. At least for a while the young girl on the road had provided me with just what I was after. God bless her.

Derek snapped open a can of lager and slurping noisily collapsed onto the opposite sofa with the type of sigh that we had both promised ourselves when we were younger we would never utter. Outside it was beginning to snow again, large goose-feather like flakes were sprinkling past the French-windows and already beginning to settle on the balcony beyond. Surely this would make it even harder for the Police to get through.

'You'd think the world had ended with the fuss the emergency services make these days,' said Derek, following my own train of thought. 'Infrastructure in this country. Slightest bit of weather and everything closes down. 'We can't come and put out your burning house because it's the wrong type of snow…' he mimicked, tutting like a Daily Mail reader.

'Well, it's only a few days after Christmas. They're probably on skeleton staff aren't they.'

'You mean they've taken one look out of the window and said 'sod that for a barrel of

soldiers,' before tucking into another mince pie.'

The whisky was good and I could feel my muscles slowly relax, sensing the same in Derek, who sighed again in that same way, an allegory of our incipient middle age. We watched the snow for a while in silence. There was something about being inside when there was an extreme of weather outside, either snow or rain, it made the contended and comfortable interior so much more so. I could even have fallen asleep had it not been for the approach of the Wicked Witches of the East and West, whose hushed whispers echoed far more obviously round the hall walls than if they'd just spoken in their normal tones.

'Alright?' asked Jude, plonking herself next to me on the sofa, whilst Soph stood by the dining table, fidgeting.

'Fine. She ok?' I said, gesturing back down the corridor.

'Fine. Still spark out, poor little thing. Wonder what happened to her.'

'Jude… shall we…' Soph said in her best whinging tone before trailing off as I shifted in my seat to look her over properly.

Jude hesitated, trying to judge what type of mood I was in, which fortunately for her was one of apathetic acknowledgement.

'Sorry I was rude before,' she said, nuzzling girlishly at my ear.

'It's fine. I don't care what you do.'

'No, I mean it. I can get a bit… carried away when I'm in a mood.'

'I said, I don't care. You were right, it's your house too. Do what you want. But the Police will be here soon.'

'We can be very discrete,' said Soph's now sultry voice, I wondered if I should ask what she meant. Jude needed no more prompting and leapt directly to her feet, skipping across the room where she and Soph tore into the small wrap like two excited schoolgirls on Christmas morning.

'Der?' called Soph over her shoulder. 'Want some?'

Derek considered his options for a polite moment or two, then deciding that he had waited long enough not to seem too eager he also got to his feet and wandered across the room, shrugging at me as he passed.

'When in Rome,' he said.

I nodded sarcastically and rolled my eyes to the ceiling despite the fact no-one was looking, and then headed toward my CD player.

'Fine then,' I said with my back turned to my friends. 'If you lot are going to be doing that, I'm putting Miles Davis on.' That would ruin their mood.

An hour later and the Police still hadn't shown up. Not that any of us cared. Those three were off their faces, vying, clawing and in Soph's case literally fighting for the attention of the group. Not that I was much better. 'A Kind of Blue' had put me in a great mood – as it always did – and the whisky helped me along the way to caring less and less about their drug fuelled antics. Despite my earlier intentions, it appeared I was actually having quite a good time.

At that exact moment Derek was clinging to the metaphorical conch shell, in mid-monologue about some rubbish or other. Losing his point he soon trailed off and Soph leapt on the opportunity to display her little party trick once again. She ignored totally what her husband had been yabbering on about, a topic that was immediately forgotten in all our collective minds, and took up her own mantle. It was as if she was halfway through an argument already, perhaps she had been having it in her head for some time, and we were all expected to keep up.

'… And a lot of the girls in the office just say they won't bother getting married at all. Don't even get the tax incentives anymore so what's the point… just carry on living in sin, init.'

I noticeably flinched when she said the word 'init'. I didn't consider myself a snob who couldn't stand such colloquial phrases (but could have been wrong); it just sounded so wrong with her Home Counties accent. So affected and contrived, those girls in the office rubbing off on her, and her not wanting to be left out of their little dialectical group. I remembered a girl I'd known at university in Liverpool in my first year. It was just myself and her from the south in our flat of ten and within less than a month she was dropping her aches and deadening her aas, I think I even heard her say 'aye' once or twice. Everyone wanted to fit in, no-one wanted to be the one left out.

Derek rolled his eyes at Soph's comments and headed

out of the room and down the hallway, presumably either to the bathroom, or out into the snow to avoid listening to her diatribe anymore. Jude wasn't listening, she had long since switched off Miles, John and the guys, had plugged in her laptop and was now flicking through her various terrible Spotify playlists, searching for something to annoy me with. I knew it was only a matter of time before '(I've had) The Time of My Life' came on and we had the same argument we always had when it did. I reached for my half full bottle and poured myself another healthy slug.

'Don't you think?' Soph continued, looking at me expectantly. Jude was engaged with her 'choones' as Soph's office mates probably would have called then, Derek had sensibly escaped, and so it was left to me to attempt acquiescence.

'Well, I don't know really know. I mean… well… we are both married, so surely that says something about what we feel about marriage as an institution.'

'Oh bollocks! I was just doing what my mother wanted me to do. Following the herd, you know. I think I married too young. They say the second time is better.'

'Who exactly is 'they'?' I asked, already knowing the answer. One of the office girls would have read it in a piece by a pseudo-feminist column writer in some trashy girlie magazine, said it to her desk neighbour and before the day was out it was gospel.

'Cosmo' wasn't it?' said Jude returning to the conversation. In the background Earth, Wind and Fire were just kicking in, this was very much the thin end of the wedge, it was all downhill from here.

'That's right,' noted Soph, grinning at me triumphantly, Jude's confirmation solidifying her point. The girls clinked glasses and knocked back the rest of their vodka & diet cokes.

'To the second time around,' toasted Jude, making eye contact with me, attempting and succeeding to rile me.

'Well, I'll be sure to pass your comments on to Derek.

Seems the pair of us are about to be let off the hook somewhat. Calls for a celebration.'

I raised my own glass, a gesture that didn't quite work as effectively with just the one.

'Just face it sad-sack,' continued Jude, warming to the theme. 'The institution of marriage is on its way out. I mean why bother anymore. We'll probably be the very last people of our age to bother tying the knot.'

'You and I clearly remember our wedding day very differently.'

'No, the wedding was great. It's just the five years since that have been the let down!'

Soph squealed with laughter and high-fived Jude before the pair of them began to dance round the living room as Madonna took over the stereo, a move which I knew it would be extremely difficult to reverse.

I sat watching them for a minute or two, sipping my whisky and attempting not to get anymore annoyed than was necessary, when I noticed my phone buzzing on the table. I stuck a finger in one ear and answered it.

'Hello?'

'*Hello. This is Police Constable Cleary.*' I waved my arm around and gestured for Jude to turn the music down, mouthing 'Police' at her. '*I just wanted to apologise that we haven't been able to get to you yet, and to let you know that we are on our way. I wanted to ask how the girl is doing?*'

'How is she doing?'

'*Yes, is there any change in her condition? As I say, we are doing everything we can to get to you as soon as possible, but as I'm sure you can appreciate the weather is making this harder than expected.*'

'Ok, well, I'll check on her and call back if there's any change.'

'*Thank you, sir.*'

After hanging up I stood and made toward the door, walking straight past a now slightly guilty looking Jude and Soph.

'What did they say?' asked Jude.

'That I've to check on her.'
'Oh right.'
'Where the hell's Derek?' asked Soph as I left the room.

Still annoyed at myself for rising to Jude's baiting I wasn't paying total attention as I pushed my way into the spare room, and so I missed exactly what happened next. On my entrance there was a flurry of movement, and then I saw Derek stood upright over the girl, whose long bare legs were now on show. She had no knickers on, a small triangle of dark brown pubic hair clearly defined and well looked after sat a few inches above her prominent vagina, which was now also quite obviously visible. Derek was clutching the corners of the covers which he then dropped back over her before making his way hurriedly across the room and past me, avoiding eye contact. I checked on the girl, who was still unconscious, but appeared stable enough, and then made my way back out to join the others, unsure of what I had just witnessed.

'She alright?' Jude asked, from where she had now positioned herself in the middle of the main sofa, just where I had been sat before.
'Fine. Where's Derek?'
'He went outside for a cigarette. Everything alright?'
'It's fine. Can you watch my phone for the Police, they should be here any minute.'
'It's called a mobile phone for a reason,' she added, but I was too distracted to argue and I crossed the room in three full strides, sliding the French-windows open and stepping out onto the snow-covered balcony where Derek stood with his back to me. I was careful to slide the door shut behind me.
'It's beautiful isn't it,' he said, meaning the snow, which covered the small park like a thick thermal blanket.
'What just happened, Derek?' I asked, struggling to keep myself calm.

Derek turned and ran his finger down the glass door where the melting snow had left a water mark.

'What do you mean?' he asked carefully.

'I mean, what were you doing to that girl, Derek? You were gone for ages.'

'I went to the toilet. Thought I should check on her, see if she was ok.'

'Then why were you so flustered when I came in? And more importantly, why did she have no trousers on?'

'I wasn't flustered. Just a little startled that you'd thrown the door open like that…'

'… Why was the door closed…?'

'… The girls must have taken her trousers off… I don't know, do I…?'

'Why was the door closed, Derek?'

He did his best to seem relaxed. A tiny smile twitched at the corner of his mouth, and he outstretched his hands, palms up, attempting to claim his innocence. But I could see there was something there that he was trying to hide. I had known him for nearly twenty years, and I knew what a terrible liar he was, guilt oozed from every pore.

'What did you do to her, Derek?'

He snorted a laugh through his nose and shook his head, still attempting to cling to that façade of innocence, but the more he tried the more it seemed to confirm my own doubts.

'Nothing! What the hell are you suggesting?'

'Well, I don't know do I. Why don't you tell me?'

Neither of us spoke for a few moments and then when it seemed he was most definitely not going to tell me I made to move back inside.

'Fine,' I said, one hand on the door handle. 'I'll just ask the girls if they took her trousers off.'

'No!' he snapped. A hand shot out and gripped my wrist. 'Please. Don't do that.'

A strange sensation started to spread through my body. It began as a nervous feeling in the pit of my belly, but quickly turned to nausea, I felt sick. I gripped the door handle harder, partly to stop the girls coming outside, and partly to stop it from shaking. Eventually I said, 'What did you do to her, Derek?'

He took his hand from my wrist and lit another cigarette, letting the smoke billow out into the evening air. At some point it had stopped snowing, I hadn't noticed.

'It's Soph.'

'Soph?'

'She… she won't, let me near her anymore.'

'What do you mean?'

'You know what I mean,' he added sharply, sucking hard on his cigarette. 'Sorry. Look, she won't let me… touch her. God knows why, she won't talk about it. We haven't… slept together in over six months, longer I think.'

'I see.'

'I honestly don't know why not. It's ever since she had this operation… I think anyway. It was just a routine thing… on her cervix. Doctor told her something but she wouldn't tell me what it was. I think… she's just paranoid she'll get infected or something, I just don't know…'

He let out a long sigh and drew again on his cigarette before flicking the butt over the edge and out of sight. I took my hand from the door handle and patted him supportively on the shoulder.

'So she won't shag you then?'

'Well if you're gonna be crude about it, then yeah. She won't shag me. Look, I had every intention of just checking on the girl, I promise. But then I looked her over and cleaned up from all the blood and stuff she looked so pretty. So young and… pure. I swear, all I did was lift the blanket and look at her. I thought she might be more comfortable without her trousers on and so I pulled them off… alright, well, there was probably some part of me that wanted to see more of her, but I… I had the best intentions… I promise. I didn't know she had no knickers on. Honest to God, or I never would have. And then you walked in.'

I let out a long sigh of my own and gripped the balcony railing with both hands, looking off into the middle distance, deciding what to do. This was my best friend. The man I had known for nearly two decades, most of my life, shared everything with, surely he wasn't capable of… of what? How much did we really know about each other? People had managed to keep whole sides of their perverted characters hidden from everyone, even their partners, for years and not get found out. Murderers and rapists got away with their crimes on a daily basis because it was often their word against someone else's, and they were willing to push it as far as it needed to go.

'And nothing happened?' I found myself asking after what felt like an eternity.

'I swear,' he said, turning to face me, desperation paining his face, his eyes pleading with me to believe him.

'Ok fine, I believe you,' I said, still unsure of what I was saying. 'But you need to get some help, buddy. Talk to someone. Start with your wife. Fucking wank more or something. Imagine if that had been the Police that opened the door at that moment.'

'Thanks bro. You're a life saver. You've got no idea how much this means to me.'

Immediately his fear was gone, replaced instead by relief, but also by something else, something I couldn't quite put my finger on, and then before I could properly work it out the French-windows flew open and Jude appeared in the doorway.

'Police are here,' she said, peering out at us, her brow furrowing as she noted the closeness of our proximity. 'Everything alright?'

'Yeah, it's fine,' I said, patting Derek on the shoulder reassuringly, steering him back toward the warmth of the inside.

Some days later and I was polishing off the last of the Glenfiddich when Jude came ambling into the front room, just as she always did, exactly when Miles was reaching the peak of a particularly piercing but equally sonorous solo.

'You should call the Police and find out what happened to that girl, you know,' she said, turning Miles off and picking up the TV remote control.

'You mean you should.'

'You are the one that dealt with them, so you do it. We should find out what happened to her. Find out if she's ok.'

I attempted to ignore her, amongst other things I was pre-empting annoyance at another bloody episode of EastEnders I was about to have to sit through.

'Just do it will you,' she went on. 'We both know I'm a lot more stubborn than you, so why don't you just do it now and save us the bother of another argument.'

I sighed and reached for my mobile, dialling the number Constable Cleary had left me, knowing I'd never hear the end of it if I didn't.

The phone was answered after the first ring.

'*Constable Cleary.*'

'Yes, hi, er… we found a girl in the street the other day, she stayed with us, and you left me your card…'

'*Ah yes. Wondering how she's doing I suppose?*'

'That's right. Is she… ok?'

'*She was admitted to A&E with some superficial facial and abdominal injuries, we think she was hit by a car…*'

Hit and run, that would make sense. Quiet, icy road, no grip, young girl unconscious, no-one around to see who did it.

'*… and internal bruising.*'

'Internal bruising?'

'*That's right. Sir, the girl you found, we think she was assaulted.*'

'Assaulted? Christ.'

At the mention of that word Jude covered her mouth

with her hand. I could already hear her repeating it to Soph on the phone in a few minutes time. She said it out loud, testing out its sound and feel, working out how to best place the inflection to get the most effective response.

'That's right, sir. We're not sure exactly when, but at some point that day, maybe the day before, we have very strong reason for thinking that someone assaulted her. I was going to contact you once the doctor has given the full prognosis, but while I have you, sir, if you saw, or heard anything at all, please let me know.'

'Ok, yes, of course, I will.'

He rang off and I placed the phone back on the coffee table, swapping it for my whisky glass, draining the rest of its contents in one. When done, I re-laid what I had just heard to Jude. She was thinking the same thing as me.

'If it was a hit and run then who the hell assaulted her? Someone just wandering by? Did you see anyone on your way back?'

'No, and no cars passed us either.'

'Strange. It doesn't make sense, does it?'

'No,' I said, my eye line wandering to the French-windows, where the iridescent streaks still lined the glass. 'It really doesn't.'

HARRY THE KILLER

It was gone 11pm by the time Harry left the Great Eastern. He stumbled slightly as he stepped out into the night, a cloud of pub fug billowing out after him into the freezing street. A hundred or so yards down the road he realised how much he needed a piss, so he stopped and relieved himself against the wall of someone's house. Upstairs a net curtain twitched, but no face appeared, and he soon slumped off again, tunelessly humming the unknown song that he had heard last.

He wondered whether he would catch Ravi's shop still open for that final final drink of the night, but thought he was probably pushing it, it was now well past 11. Too late even for Ravi. Turning the corner back onto Lower Marsh Road Harry was plunged into darkness as the streetlamps did not continue around the corner. The traffic noise soon faded away too, and within only a hundred yards or so the only sound was that of Harry's own foot fall and his heavy breathing. Nothing he wasn't used to. How many times had he made this short journey over the years? A thousand? Two?

Then slowly he became aware of another set of feet, falling on the firm concrete just out of synch with his own. He could not see anyone on the straight road up ahead and a quick glance over his shoulder told him that there was no-one behind him. He kept walking and the other footsteps continued too. Quite suddenly he stopped, trying to catch the owner of the other footsteps out, but the sound immediately stopped too. He turned but still could not make anyone out on the street behind him. He must be making it up, he told himself, and carried on walking. Harry had lived in London a long time and was fully aware of how important it was to keep your wits about you, especially after a few drinks, so he quickened his pace, the other footsteps quickening in time with his.

Back within the safety of the flat building he hung by the main door for a few moments, but there was no-one on the street outside. The area silent for the night. He tried to tell himself that he must have imagined it, or it was just an echo or something, but couldn't shake the feeling that someone was watching him. By the time he reached his front door, situated on the dimly lit third floor, the feeling was subsiding. He reached for his keys and placed them in the door, taking a furtive glance up and down the hallway first. He very nearly didn't see it before entering the house, but something different about the front door caught his eye and he stopped. There, pinned to the door on a typical piece of lined A4 paper, in bold, capital letters, were written the words 'HARRY THE KILLER'.

A few nights later, when Harry was no longer working nights, he thought about going to the pub again. The warm, welcoming space, complete with an array of alcoholic drinks to help him ignore life, was drawing him, but then he remembered the footsteps and the note and thought twice about it. Who the hell was it? Surely no-one knew about his past. He had never told anyone about that one, stupid mistake he had made more than twenty years ago when he was still in the army. Was it just bloody kids? He'd never had trouble like that before though, and the writing was non-descript to the point of clinical, so unlikely to be made by a young hand. Certainly not the kids that lived on this estate. He told himself it was nothing, just some stupid prank he wasn't in on, and grabbed his coat, no chance he was going to miss out on the pub because of some tomfoolery.

By the time he walked through the doors of the Great Eastern some ten-to-fifteen minutes later he felt the eyes of the assembled few on him, and he half expected them to start sniggering. Had it been them that had left the note as some kind of practical joke he didn't get? No-one laughed though and within a few strides he was across the pub floor and pulling himself onto his favourite stool, nodding at the other regulars.

Young Jimmy soon appeared behind the bar. 'Alright Harry,' he said. 'Usual?'

Harry nodded and began to feel better after the first couple of sips. Then with each new sip, the note and the footsteps were pushed further from his mind. One pint turned into two, and then three, and soon he fell into conversation with Jock and Sammy. Only once was he reminded of his experience the other night, and that was when Jock told them about how his daughter had been followed home.

'What happened?' Harry had asked, perhaps too abruptly. 'Did they catch the guy?'

'It was her ex,' said Jock, slightly taken aback at Harry's out of character eager concern. 'Police had a word and that was that. Ain't heard from him since.'

It was clearly not the same person and Harry went back to his pint, attempting to regain his usual air of nonchalance.

Come closing time and he was out on the street again, unable to shake the feeling that his experience was going to be repeated. After the first few steps down the high street, he was confident that no-one was following him, there being the usual scattering of late-night folk also making their way home, and cars and buses swooshing past on the slick, damp street. Then as he turned once more onto Lower Marsh Road, and the sounds of the high street once again faded into the background, the distinct clip clop of another set of footsteps fell into line behind him. He tried to remember his army training, but it had been such a long time ago he wasn't sure what to do, so he told himself to breathe deeply and stay calm. Then suddenly he stopped walking, but the other footsteps kept going. Gotcha! Without thinking he spun round and made a grab into thin air. Stood a few yards back was Jimmy, the young bartender from the pub. He stopped as Harry flung himself about.

'Harry!' he said, startled by Harry's actions. 'You alright, mate?'

Harry stood still, feeling slightly foolish, but not letting himself be dissuaded. Was Jimmy the one that was following him? Had he left the note?

'Jimmy,' he said, keeping himself as calm as he could. 'Where are you going?'

'Home.'

'Not seen you round here before? Don't you live over the river?'

'Er… yeah,' said Jimmy, fidgeting with his hands, taking a measured step back. 'My missus. She lives in the block of flats there.' He pointed up at Harry's flat block. Was his hand shaking? It was hard to tell.

'Right,' said Harry, still unsure.

'Right. See you then.'

Jimmy set off down the road, past Harry and toward the flat block. Harry stood and watched as he buzzed one of the flats from outside and then stepped past the door when he was let in. Was he following him? Harry wasn't sure and felt a bit silly for acting the way he had done, but then he noticed that he heard no other footsteps on the street as he made his way down the rest of the road.

As he reached his floor, he was beginning to wonder whether perhaps he might have imagined it all, when he saw from the end of the hallway that there was something pinned to his door. He stopped, feeling the blood drain from his face and his heart suddenly beating hard against his chest. He forced himself on, straining to make out the writing, wishing for it to be a note from his neighbour, but knowing it wasn't. As he drew near enough to make out the words he stopped again, this time leaning over the side railing, catching his breath, nearly throwing up into the London night.

In the same, clinical black, capital letters, the note read: 'HARRY AND MILO WOZ ERE, '93'.

The days tumbled by and Harry soon began not to notice the footsteps that clip clopped down the road after him, so concerned as he was about finding another note. And soon enough it was more likely that he would find a fresh, new piece of paper complete with a brand-new message pinned to the door as he turned the corner to his floor, than not. The sight of each one filled him with a horribly familiar feeling of dread and nausea, and soon he asked his boss for more night shifts, so it was daylight when he returned home.

Each one was different but centred around the same theme: 'HARRY THE KILLER RESIDES BEHIND THIS DOOR'; 'HARRY AND MILO WOZ MATES, WHERE'S MILO NOW?'; and the most blunt: 'HARRY KILLED MILO'. He was scared to ask his neighbours about the notes because if they had read them, what did they think of him, and were they going to shop him? But he forced himself to in case they had seen who had done it. Everyone liked to turn a blind eye to most activity on this estate, but the fact that not one person had seen one single note being stuck to the door both scared and mystified Harry, and soon enough he realised there was only one thing for it, he was going to have to confront his past.

Harry and Milo were great mates in the army. They had started on exactly the same day and were born in the same year. They were evenly matched physically, and encouraged by their squad sergeants, soon everything was turned into a competition. Whether it be cross country running, or peeling potatoes in the mess, one of them would eventually claim victory over the other one and hold it over him until they found the next thing to compete over. They kept score with a tally chart, written on an old scrap of A4 paper that they hung up on the space between their beds.

One day when they were out swimming in the river estuary, what was supposed to be a relaxing session for the squad, quickly turned into a 'who can swim to the other side first' competition between the two young privates, and they had taken off, side by side, their sergeant's words about rip tides and strong undercurrents falling on deaf ears. When they were nearly halfway across, Milo had slowly begun to pull ahead of Harry, and despite how much extra he had tried to dig into his reserves, Harry could feel that he wasn't going to catch him. A sudden rage coursed through his body, this would be the third competition in a row that he was going to lose, and he could already see Milo's stupid grin. Without thinking, he had lashed out, his hand catching Milo's Achilles Tendon with a solid thump. Milo had shrieked and stopped swimming just long enough for Harry to pull past him and into the lead. Knowing that Milo would now redouble his efforts, Harry hadn't dared look back and had made it to the other side first, pulling himself exhausted but ecstatic from the water. Milo was nowhere to be seen. Harry swam back out and under the surface but couldn't find him anywhere.

It later transpired that he had been caught in an undercurrent and swept out to sea, washing up lifeless on a beach, twenty miles away, a few days later. Harry had been reprimanded for reclass action, but he had never told a soul about lashing out at Milo's ankle. He had very nearly done, drunk at Milo's funeral. He had wanted to tell Milo's bereaved girlfriend, whisky and guilt pounding his head, but he hadn't. He was sure he hadn't. Had he?

In his flat one morning, after another long night shift, and now about halfway into a bottle of scotch, Harry was as usual thinking about who it was that was leaving the notes. They even seemed to know when he was home, and nothing appeared if he failed to leave the house all day.

On a whim he pulled out the old carboard box he kept

at the back of his wardrobe that contained his old army stuff and started to flick through the contents. He came across the letters that Milo had written to him when he'd had a month away from the barracks one summer, and Harry sat down to read them. It was like Milo was back in the room again, and Harry couldn't help the tears that sprung up in his eyes. Why hadn't he told anyone about what he did? It probably wouldn't have made any difference, but surely it would have made him feel better. Surely? No. All it would have done is give him a dishonourable discharge and maybe even a stint inside, no hope of a future.

And then he came across a section in a letter that reminded him of why Milo had been off for that time. It was his girlfriend. She had had a baby. It had been unexpected, and because they were so young, and the baby had been premature, Milo had been given special leave. It had been a baby boy. Small, but healthy. Harry stopped reading, his head swimming from the booze. Everything had fallen into place. There it was in Milo's scruffy handwriting, 'We've decided to call him James. After my granddad. Maybe Jamie for short, or even… Jimmy.'

The following night Harry was back in the pub claiming his favourite seat once more after something of an extended absence.

'Good to see you back,' said Si, the landlord, placing a pint in front of Harry.

'Cheers. Young Jimmy about tonight?' asked Harry.

'Yeah, he'll be here in a minute.'

When Jimmy had arrived, Harry had done his best not to look like he knew his secret, whilst also watching his every move to gauge his reaction to Harry's reappearance in the pub. If he was at all surprised that Harry had made it back, he did a good job of not showing it.

Twenty minutes before closing time Harry said his goodbyes and left the pub, making sure Jimmy had seen him go. Rather than walking home though, he waited around the corner. Jimmy emerged a while later and set off down the road, clearly heading for Harry's block of flats. 'Girlfriend, my arse,' Harry thought to himself, and set off after him.

Back on Lower Marsh Road, Harry had done his best to fall in time with Jimmy's footsteps, staying about five yards behind him. Jimmy made it about halfway down before turning to see who it was walking so closely behind him. Harry was ready, and he sprung forward, pushing Jimmy hard up against the wall, producing a bread knife from beneath his jacket.

'Think it's funny do you! Eh,' he screamed, the knife against Jimmy's throat. 'Following old men and leaving them creepy notes about your dad, eh, do ye!'

His intention had been just to scare him, show him that he wouldn't be taken advantage of, but he could feel the months of latent rage building up inside him, and he was unable to stop it.

'Harry!' gasped Jimmy. 'What's going on?? I haven't done anything, mate…'

Harry took the knife away from his throat, but the rage didn't subside. He leaned forward as close as he dared and with a low, firm voice said, 'Stop the notes, yeah. Just leave it. I never meant to kill your dad, it was a long time ago, now just leave it, right?'

With that he pushed himself off and let Jimmy go, taking a step back, ready to leave. If only Jimmy had stayed silent.

'My dad? What you talking about Harry? My dad's not…'

But Harry didn't let him finish, instead he was given all the provocation that he needed, and like a flash he turned and plunged the bread knife deep into Jimmy's belly, pulling it out in one fluid motion. Jimmy looked at the knife, then at Harry, and then slowly began to drop to the floor.

'Harry! What have you done, mate?' he wailed, his voice quivering, his body going into shock. 'You've got to call an ambulance, mate…'

But Harry was not around to hear him. He had placed the bread knife back in his jacket pocket and slumped off down the empty street toward home, Jimmy's muffled cries of pain lost in the evening breeze.

It was a few weeks later that Harry began to finally relax again. The Police had knocked on his door asking if he had seen or heard anything, but just like the other thousand or so residents on the estate, he hadn't heard a thing. Harry had switched back to day shifts, to the annoyance of his boss, and better than that, the notes had stopped too. He must have been right after all, Jimmy was Milo's son and his strange idea about twisted revenge had backfired. He hadn't meant to kill Jimmy, he knew that. He had just been pushed too far by the notes prank and had acted, through his ingrained army training, in the heat of the moment. It was all done now, and there was no point in dwelling on it further. Harry was free to carry on enjoying his neighbourhood at night.

On his way back from the pub one night, having timed it right to nip into Ravi's on the way home, Harry found himself in a better mood than he had for some time. The worst of winter was over and there was even something of the feel of spring in the air. He was therefore lost in his thoughts as he turned the corner to his floor again and nearly failed to notice something pinned to his front door. Just like that, he was back in that place once more, the terror returning to the pit of his stomach as the blood drained from his face. He found himself rooted to the spot, but forced himself on, knowing he had to read the note, knowing it was inevitable.

As he drew closer he looked away, over the balcony and out into London, anywhere that meant not looking at the note, but before long he was outside his flat and he forced himself to look.

It read in that same clinical, black handwriting: 'HARRY THE KILLER'. It was a basic replica of the first ever note, accept this time there was something else added to it, something that Harry could have sworn was not there the first time. Two vertical marks had been drawn in the bottom left-hand corner, two marks that looked like the beginning of a tally chart.

FIRST TIME; LAST TIME

At the time it felt like I was woken by a scream, but I later thought it more likely to be the sudden silence. The absence of sound. A cursory gust of wind dying away, or the quiet that followed the final exodus from the pub car park further down the street. The alarm clock told me it was 2:07am. I had been asleep for more than three hours but felt as awake as if it were 7am and time to get ready for school. I don't know what drew me from my bed, but I threw back the duvet and stepped out into the room, careful not to wake my younger brother, who was breathing gently on the top bunk. It was mid-winter, and the large, high-ceilinged Victorian room was often colder than outside, the damp in the highest corner spreading lethargically across the ceiling; but I ignored the chill and padded barefoot across the worn carpet in just my nightie, side stepping Dom's toy soldiers as I approached the window. I reached up with a shivering arm that could have belonged to someone else and drew back the curtain just a few inches.

Outside, the full moon cast an uneasy, luminous glow across the half of the back garden visible from the house. The safety light blinked on as the lightest breeze threw a handful of leaves tumbling past the back door, illuminating the garden shed that directly faced the house. Something was different. What was it? It took a few moments but then I realised that the door to the shed was shut. Not locked as it sometimes was from the outside, but closed and held in place by something, or someone, on the inside. It couldn't be shut like that without being locked in place, and it had been open when I had gone to bed, the door creaking back and forth on its hinges, audible and nearly keeping me from falling asleep. Nearly.

My dressing gown was on the back of the bedroom door, but I ignored it despite the night chill and instead gingerly opened the door, careful not to allow it the creek it always had in the last six inches. The landing was in complete darkness, the moon over the other side of the building at this time of night, but I could have navigated the whole house with my eyes shut and I descended the stairs as quiet as a ghost trapped between worlds, laboriously ascending and descending the stairs, a spectral Sisyphus.

The tiled kitchen floor was made of black and white squares like a chess board, and I was the tiny pawn valiantly heading toward an unlikely victory or near certain doom, the numbers steeply against me. Afterwards I would tell my mother how I had missed the letter left propped up by the vase of lilies, set in the middle of the huge oak dining table my parents had inherited twenty years before, the darkness and my eagerness to get outside driving me forward.

The garden was as calm as it always seemed to feel on Christmas Day, when the elements that so often disturbed the garden seemed to take a rest so that Dom and I could play with our new toys. The moon must have disappeared behind a cloud because I was plunged into darkness as I stepped outside, away from the comfort of the house. My presence switched the security light on though, its sudden yellowy-orange glow brightening the chilly blackness of the night and lighting the way ahead of me, showing me my route forwards, leading the way.

Finally, I noticed the cold. My naked feet quickly numbing on the stones of the clumsily laid garden path that led up to the shed and past it, down to the end of the garden where we would bring our friends to play when we were younger.

I took a few hesitant steps forward and then a few more, juxta-posing feelings of confidence and apprehension battling it out as I neared the shed. My mind was blank. Afterwards, with hindsight, I would embellish different versions of the truth, telling people that part of me knew what I was going to find, but if I was honest, I thought of nothing as my hand reached up, just as it had done moments before at the bedroom window. This time though I knew it was my arm and I knew what I was doing. Perhaps I did know, perhaps that wasn't a lie, perhaps I just couldn't face the truth while living it. It had seemed so obvious afterwards, back in the warmth of the house, the emotions pushed so deeply down it would be years before they would be properly dealt with, but at the time the only thing I could think was that my hand wasn't shaking. It should have been. Just because of the night chill if nothing else, but it wasn't.

The door wouldn't give. The padlock lay abandoned on the ground a few feet away, as if it would never be needed again, the keys hanging meaninglessly from it. I tugged at the door once more, but it stayed fast. I wasn't dissuaded though and reached up with both hands, awkwardly slotting my fingers into a gap between the door and the frame in lieu of a handle. Suddenly it gave way, and something lurched out at me as the door flew open. I jumped back as the spade that had been wedged up against the door clattered to the ground in front of me. I stared at it for a few moments, then my eyeline was drawn slowly up to the darkness of the doorway. I was suddenly aware of my heart beating a slow and steady pace, hard against my chest, speeding up as my eyes grew accustomed to the dark and I slowly began to make out the shape of my father hanging from the ceiling of the shed. It wasn't fear that froze me to the spot. It wasn't the cold either. I just couldn't move. I couldn't make out his features either, but for some reason when I remember that moment back, I see him smiling down at me. Free at last, perhaps. Mother and everyone else would tell me that it was for the best that I couldn't make out his face. They would take charge of my emotions and actions over the coming days, and I would feature in body alone, told what to do, and how to feel.

The other thing I remember in that moment was slowly becoming aware of something on the inside of my thigh. There was a thin dark trail leading down the top of my left leg, red staining the front of my nightie. My first period. I had come of age in the time I had been stood there. What would he have said? I had a vision of him looking away out of awkwardness and private disgust.

As it turned out, this would be the last time that I would see my father. (Mother didn't want an open casket at the funeral.) Not the few hours earlier when I had chanced on him sat in his study staring aimlessly at the wall, but now, hanging from a handmade noose, swinging in slow concentric circles above the unfinished pot plants and bags of unused cement mix.

Sometime later I wondered why I didn't try to cut him down. Or at least check if he was dead. He was, but should I have checked? Someone would ask me this when I finally went back to school, and I would admit that I didn't know. Too scared? Too weak and small at just thirteen years old? Both? Instead, I just stood there and watched him, swaying gently back and forth, his problems finally over; ours, just beginning. First time; last time. It was peaceful for a while, and then slowly the ominous feeling that I should tell someone began to filter through my body, and I turned and shuffled slowly back to the house, knowing that as soon as I woke my mother nothing would ever be the same again. I wondered how long I could wait for.

FAMILY TIES

I'd just left mother's house when I first bumped into her. Colin had some papers he wanted to give me, research he had done years before that he thought would help with my latest venture, a book on the all too short reign of Edward VI. Mother had fussed as usual with tea and cakes as Colin had walked me through the newspaper articles and notes that must have dated back fifty years. To be honest it was more bumph than use but it never hurts to make one's retired stepfather feel of use.

She was walking her dog and as I turned the corner of Liberty road, I became somehow entangled in the lead. The tiny terrier, scared by the sudden appearance of my shin heading toward its face, attempted to escape from the entanglement by yelping and yanking as hard as it could, which in turn caused me to lose my balance and the whole lot of us ended up in a mixed pile on the corner of the street, me attempting to prevent the barking dog from biting a hole in the arm of my blazer.

Over tea and crumpets at her rather grand apartment just round the corner on Bridge Street Gardens we finally saw the funny side of it.

'So, you're a writer then, Neil?' she asked, sipping from her ornate bone-china teacup and smiling warmly. She had the type of smile that swims over you, makes you feel immediately like you are being cared for, and the kind of look in her eyes that shows she is always listening to what you say, not merely waiting for her turn to talk.

'Well, I don't know about a writer really, Deirdre,' I replied, eyeing the long thin pieces of short bread, the expensive stuff you got from Marks. 'I'm a Historian really, but I've taken to writing books, just to keep me out of the classroom if I'm honest. The older I get the less I like to deal with the younger generation.'

'Fascinating,' she went on. 'I dabbled with pen and

paper myself, in my youth anyway, mostly romantic nonsense really, nothing of any substance, certainly nothing a man of your stature would be interested in.'

'You'll have to let me read your work sometime.'

She smiled again. 'Help yourself to short bread,' she added.

We arranged to meet at the British Museum at the end of the week so I could walk her round the Hadrian exhibition. She was a fan apparently but had not had the chance to attend yet. I offered to buy the tickets, being a Friend I could get in for free.

'And do accept my apologies for Sebastian,' she said, showing me to the door. 'He can get so carried away at times. Hates to think he can't escape. Can't be caged too long that one. Make sure to send me the bill for your dry cleaning.'

I went to the library to continue my research but could not focus properly. Whenever I started to read anything her sweet smile would slip back into my thoughts and I found myself idly dreaming of what it would be like to sit with her on the same sofa, witness her break into that smile as I read her an article in the evening paper, or catch her glance as I answered a question on University challenge correctly. Sweet, sweet Deirdre.

'Well, she's about the same age as Margaret, I suppose.'

'And what colour's her hair?'

'Do you really need to know that mum?'

'What's that? No Colin, he won't tell me. What's that? Colin asks why you're being so secretive about your new lady friend.'

'She's hardly my new lady friend, mum, I'm taking her to the British Museum, it's not even a proper date.'

'What? Oh yeah. Colin asks, when can we meet her?'

'Mum! You can't meet her.'

'Why not?'

'I've only just met her. You don't take someone to

meet your parents on a first date.'

'But you said it wasn't a date.'

'Mum, please, I'm not bringing her to meet you.'

'What? Colin says is she prettier than Margaret?'

'Prettier than Margaret? Oh, I don't know. Maybe. I don't know. I split up with Margaret a long time ago mum. I've been on my own for almost ten years.'

'What about that Belgian girl? You were with her, weren't you? The one with the big hair. Brought her on holiday to Majorca with us, didn't you?'

'Yes, I did mum, but that wasn't really anything proper. I mean, we were only together three months or something… it was… well… that was a long time ago as well…'

'What? I'll ask. Colin asks is she prettier than the Belgian girl?'

'Bye, mum.'

She suggested we go to the exhibition in the early afternoon to avoid the crowds. She was a retired primary school teacher, and I could miss an afternoon of research – the beauty of being one's own boss – and so we met on the forecourt of the British Museum a little after 2 o'clock. She was wearing a purple knee length dress that would not have looked out of place on the Queen in the mid-seventies, and the same long white coat I had seen her wear the first time we had met. She clutched a purple handbag to her bosom with her left hand, the other constantly checking her hair which she wore in a tight bun. Thankfully, the dog was nowhere to be seen.

Given her apparel I was glad to have chosen the smarter of my blazers, the navy blue one with the dark gold buttons I had made sure to polish that very morning, completed by my lightly tanned chinos, white shirt and the navy-blue tie mother had given me for Christmas.

'Oh, you do look smart,' she said, running a hand up my lapel, a movement that sent a slight alien feeling rushing through my stomach. 'Just like a sailor.'

'Why thank you. My father was a sailor.'

'Oh really? I would love to meet him one day, I loved to sail.'

'He died when I was very little actually.'

'Oh, I am sorry.'

'Please, how were you to know. I never really knew him to be honest. I was raised by my mother and a very loving step-father.'

'A step-father. How rare for people… our age… to be raised by a stepfather. And they are both still around, are they?'

'Very much so. In fact, I was coming from their house the other day when we first bumped into each other.'

'Really? On Pontefract terrace? Which number, I know a few people on that street.'

'Number 14. Colin and Gladys Chilvers. Do you know them?'

'Afraid not,' she said, breaking eye contact for just a second before looking up and smiling once more. 'But I'm sure I will.'

After the exhibition – which I am glad to say provided me with the perfect opportunity to play the guide; her asking plenty of questions and me giving carefully pre-prepared answers – we found ourselves a seat in the little café in the top hand corner of the Great Court. She had a cup of Earl Grey, black, and I the same but with slim-line milk.

'And are your parents still with us?' I asked after we had done all the talk we could do on ancient Rome without it turning into an undergraduate tutorial, and there seemed nothing else for me to ask.

'Oh no. My mother died a long time ago. I inherited the house from her actually.'

'It's very nice. And your father?'

'My father? Oh, I never knew my father. I think he died before I was born… at least, that's what mother had me believe.

'I am sorry to hear that. I… I hope you don't mind me asking you this but… did… did you ever marry?'

She held out her slim left hand which was covered in just the lightest splattering of liver spots, and looked at the vacant spot on her ring finger.

'Marry. No. Never. But… never say never…'

I felt my cheeks burn a deep dark crimson, but feeling a fire lit inside me I found the courage to carry on.

'Deirdre. I was wondering if you would do me the pleasure of allowing me to escort you to dinner, this evening.'

'Why Neil. It would be my pleasure.'

'Smashing.'

That evening I arrived ten minutes early to her flat and waited diligently on the corner until the allotted time, hoping I was out of sight, so she wouldn't think I was lurking. Something did not feel quite right though, there were no lights on in her house. Her sitting room looked out over the road and the curtains were wide open, even though it was pitch black out on the street. In fact, there was no sign of life at all. I rang the doorbell but gave up after ten minutes, wondering what had happened. I had said 8 o'clock, hadn't I? I was sure I had. Where on earth could she be?

I hung around for a further fifteen minutes and then reluctantly gave up, wandering slowly down the street checking over my shoulder to see if the lights had sparked on at the last second, but alas there was no sign. How very strange.

Returning home, I dialled the number she had given me, written on the back of a British Museum postcard, perhaps she had fallen asleep, or worse, had a fall. The answerphone clicked in after five rings.

'Hi Deirdre, it's… it's Neil. I've just come from your flat. I am fairly sure I was due to er… to er… pick you up at 8 o'clock, must have been my mistake. Silly old fool, always getting things like that mixed up. Perhaps you could give me a call when you get this message, I'm… er… most dreadfully sorry.'

And then after a moment's pause, I called mother's number. Engaged. Typical, probably talking to that Ethel. Only lives next door, quite why they need to talk on the phone as well I'll never know.

I made a cup of tea but left it on the side, instead opting for a drop of Brandy. I sat on the sofa and turned on the TV but felt too restless to watch it so switched it quickly off, instead opting for another Brandy and a pace of the front room. I just could not sit still or concentrate on anything. Should I call the police? What if she had that fall, she could be really hurt, or even worse! No, I told myself, she would be fine. Either I had got the time wrong, or she had double booked. It was all just so strange. She had seemed so keen that afternoon.

I called mother again. Still engaged. After a further Brandy and two more failed attempts to first watch the TV and then read a book I decided on a walk.

My feet lead my rather instinctively to mother's house. I knocked on the heavy oak door and again gained no response. I looked at my watch, it was a little after 9, they were never out later than 9pm, and never in bed before 11pm. I banged again, louder in case the TV was on too high a volume. Still no response. There was certainly something fishy going on.

I made my way around the back of the house to where I knew the backdoor would be open. The handle slipped seamlessly down, and as I stepped over the threshold, I made the same mental note I always did to remind them to lock their back door, anyone could get in through it. The sound of the TV was loud from the front room which in turn made me sigh in relief, they must have missed the doorbell, strange though, it would be the first time that had ever happened.

'Only me, mum,' I called, pushing the door to the living room open. 'You know, you really should lock that back door, anyone could…'

I froze.

'What the…?' I managed after what seemed like an eternity had passed.

There before me were mother and Colin sat in the middle of the three-seater sofa, clutching each other, their faces shining white with terror and their eyes so wide I could make out the little red veins running into the pupils on either side. On the rug in front of the gas fire lying on his back was Sebastian the terrier, a long gash running from his neck, down his chest and ending halfway through his stomach, blood seeped from the wound, slowly soaking into the already dark crimson rug my mother had bought in Morocco two summer's back.

'What on earth is going on?' I asked my mother and Colin, my voice notably shaking. They both looked my way but neither spoke, instead Colin's eyes flickered back to the other figure in the room.

She held a large knife out in front of her. What I hoped was only Sebastian's blood dripped from the end. The sweet smile that I had fallen so heavily for was now replaced with a deep routed scowl of the sort I had never seen before. Those beautifully inquisitive eyes nothing more than pin pricks in a wild-eyed stare.

'You must be my step-brother then,' said Deirdre.

'Step… what…?'

'Colin here is my father. He abandoned me and my mother when I was just three years old. Didn't you Colin,' she spat out his name and made a gesture toward the sofa, causing mother and step-father to flinch in unison. 'He fell for your bitch of a mother who wouldn't let him see his old family, the daughter he never knew, and the wife he always hated. Well mother couldn't handle it, she killed herself. And you didn't even come to the funeral, did you…!'

'Colin is your… father? But… you told me your father died.'

'I lied Neil. I needed to find out where they lived, and you were only too eager to tell me, weren't you. Men are so easy to play. Flutter your eyelids, listen to their boring stories about Hadrian and they are putty in your hands. Pathetic really.'

'But. You said you liked Hadrian!' That one cut deep, but I pushed on, there was questions to be asked. 'How did you know I was their son?'

'I didn't. I knew they had a son, and what age he was. I… had to 'accidentally' bump into every man on this street and take them for tea. I've wasted my inheritance looking for you…!' She moved suddenly forward, and my mother screamed, I stepped toward her, not quite sure what I planned to do but as I did, she moved the knife in my direction instead, stopping short of the sofa.

'You stay there… brother…'

'But I don't understand,' I said. 'Why… why did you kill your dog…?'

'That dog. That type of dog. A terrier,' said Colin's hollow voice. 'That was the only present I ever bought her.'

'That's right,' added Deirdre. 'Sebastian was the third one of them I've had in my hunt for Daddy.

'But… but that doesn't make any sense… listen Deirdre, I think you need help…'

'NONE OF THIS MAKES ANY SENSE YOU FOOL!' she bellowed, shaking the knife in my direction, myself, mother and Colin all flinched back at the movement, my back hit the wall. Across the room the curtains were closed against the street and I could see the phone lying off the hook. My mobile, hardly ever used, was sat in my pocket; if only I could reach it, maybe I could call the police.

'So,' I began carefully, reaching slowly into my left

pocket and feeling the cold unfamiliar lump of plastic. There was a bump on the 5, which meant the 9 was directly down and to the right, I pressed it three times. 'What exactly do you plan on doing now?'

'That,' she said, breaking her look from her father and turning to point the knife my way once more, 'is indeed a good question. I hadn't quite planned this far ahead… but… I'm sure I'll think of something…'

BRIEF ENCOUNTER

It was 6 o'clock on Friday evening and I was in a bar, sat on a stool, a double Jack Daniels in front of me.

'Anyone sitting there?' said a voice from somewhere behind me.

'Not that I know of,' I said, but didn't look up.

'Thanks,' added the voice, and then after a pause continued with, 'Are you ok?'

I glanced over at a rather plain faced girl with an American accent who had sat on the stool next to mine. She beamed back at me.

'I'm fine,' I said, not smiling, and then looked away.

'Well, you don't look fine.'

I turned again, this time inspecting her closer, she'd pulled off the large purple bobble hat she'd been wearing to reveal a stock of short red, wiry hair, which she ran her hands pointlessly through.

'Not that it's any business of yours but I'm just here for a quiet drink and don't want to be disturbed with idle small talk if it's all the same to you,' I spat out, my tone perhaps a little bit sharper than I'd intended.

'Oh, I see.'

She paused and then turned away from me back to the bar, signalling in vain for the bartender.

And that was just what I didn't want. The heavy feeling of guilt brought on by my being rude to a perfect stranger. As if I didn't have enough things on my conscience to worry about as it was. If I was going to lose myself in my solitude and wallow in self-pity then I'd have to apologise.

'Look I'm sorry,' I said. 'I've just had some bad news today and I wanted a quiet drink, I didn't mean to snap.'

'It's ok,' she said, still trying to signal to the bartender, who stood idly chatting with a waitress by the door to the kitchen. 'I'm sorry for disturbing you.'

I looked back at the double Jack Daniels I hadn't yet

touched. The girl muttered something that I didn't quite hear.

'Sorry?'

'What? Oh nothing, I was just wondering what the hell I had to do to get a drink in this place.'

I stood on the rail alongside the bottom of the bar and leaned far over the side, waving my arm as I did.

'Hey mate,' I called, catching the bartender's attention, 'can we get a drink up here!'

He sauntered slowly up to us and leaned heavily on the edge of the bar.

'It's a skill,' I said to her, she glared back at me, unimpressed.

'What can I get you?' the bartender said, a thick Italian accent giving away his roots.

'What would you like?'

'White wine and soda please. Do you want anything?'

I gestured to my full glass. 'Not for me thanks.'

She paid for her drink and sipped tentatively from it, as if it was a steaming mug of tea. I glanced again at my own drink and wondered for the millionth time since I'd been here what to do with it.

'You not going to drink that?' she said, nodding at my full glass.

'I'm considering it.' I finally forced a smile.

'You must be a cheap date.'

And she was right. For the past three years I had been a cheap date, and for the 6 years before that I certainly had not been, or a particularly pleasant date either. In all honesty I wasn't quite sure what had driven me into a bar after all this time. It could have been the fact that I'd recently split from Gloria, co-habiting girlfriend of two years, within the last 20 minutes, but then I had been through worse in the last three years and hadn't turned to the bottle then, the death of my father topping that particular list.

Perhaps it was the fact that I was alone now and could

do what I wanted. She wasn't standing over me any longer, making sure I did the right thing, acting the right way, telling me off when I didn't. It was true, as soon as I'd got off the phone from her I'd headed straight for the nearest bar, letting age old instinct lead the way. Clouded and maybe even comfortable in the fact that I could finally do what I wanted without having to let someone else know where I was all the time. She certainly didn't appreciate being called a parole officer checking up on me on the phone twenty-five minutes before. But then what girl would? I hoped that my will power and self-control came from my own inner strength, and not from the fear of disappointing the person that I loved and looked after me.

'Would you mind if I called you a parole officer?' I said to the girl. She'd produced a well-thumbed paperback which she had spread out on the bar in front of her, just about to start reading.

'A parole officer?'

'Yes. Would you mind if I called you one?'

'Erum, why would you do that?'

'Well let's just say that I did. Would you mind?'

'Mind? Erum… well I suppose not, there's worse things you could call me. But then, I suppose it depends upon the context really.'

'You see, that's just what I thought.'

She sighed and closed the book, turning slightly so that she half-faced me.

'What's happened then?' she said.

'Oh no. I don't want to interrupt. I'm sorry for disturbing you, you get back to your book.'

'Look, I don't think I could sit here with you thinking so loudly next to me and still be able to concentrate on my book anyway, so you might as well tell me.'

'In that case, I just split up with my girlfriend.'

'Yup, thought as much. And any normal red-blooded male would already be slaughtered by now. So why aren't you?'

'Can't you guess?'

'I think I probably can, but in my experience it always benefits to say it out loud.'

'What are you some kind of councillor or something?'

'Yes, I am as a matter of fact, and normally I charge £200 an hour for this type of consultation. Back in the states it would have been double that.'

'I see. Well lucky me then. Who would have thought I'd find the answer to all my problems in a bar, eh.'

'That's called irony.'

I laughed and glanced at my drink. Suddenly it didn't seem as tempting as it previously had.

'I shouldn't have to burden you with my problems when you've just come here for a quiet drink though.'

'Just get on with it will you.'

'Oh, lovely bedside manner.'

'You're getting the economy version, which will include kicking and screaming if I so wish. You want tender loving care and free coffee you come and see me on a weekday in my office, call my secretary to make an appointment.'

She smiled, just so I knew that she was not being entirely serious.

'Well,' I started, memories of past discussion groups and personal therapy sessions flooding back to me. 'I am a recovering alcoholic. I haven't touched a drink for over two years now.'

'You must be thirsty.'

I looked down at the JD once more.

'Do you know, not as much as I thought I'd be.'

'No, I meant…'

'I know. It's fine. Funny thing is I think it was just natural instinct that led me here today. I don't think I even *wanted* a drink, I didn't even think about it, it just kind of… happened. Back when I was drinking if anything ever went wrong, which got more and more frequent near the end, then I'd just head for the nearest pub to help take the pain away. They say you drink to forget, but all I did was sit at the bar thinking about whatever the problem was, it certainly didn't help it go away. I probably would've been better off playing football or doing a degree or something to help take my mind off it.'

'Sounds like you're cured.'

'Ha! No, seriously, tell me what you think, I'd appreciate your thoughts.'

'Well, the whole point of counselling is to let the person talk for themselves. Find their way through the problem and come up with their own conclusions. But it sounds like you know what you're talking about. People drink because it's safe for them, they know where they are with a pint in their hand, and they know what it'll do to them. However, it is also a drug that your body can come dependent upon if you take too much of it. That's when it is not even your choice whether to drink or not anymore, it's not up to your conscious mind, and that's when you need to get medical help. Was it ever that bad with you?'

I sat back on my stool and took a slow look around the bar. It was Friday evening and people were relaxing into their weekend, chatting amicably in groups or couples, stood up or at tables, tucked away in corners or out on display in the middle of the place. Everyone seemed so happy. The distinction I'd never been able to make was whether that happiness came from the alcohol that they were pumping into their bodies, or whether the drink was just a by-product and was merely helping to enhance their evening. I had never been able to enjoy an evening without a drink and had never known when I had had too many. I had always just tried to fit as much alcohol into my body as I could in the shortest possible period of time, slaving under the misapprehension that I was having a good time.

'I am not sure if I was ever physically reliant upon it,' I said, remembering the weekend I had spent shivering even in the brilliant sunshine on a camping trip Gloria's short-lived predecessor had forced me to go on.

'Really?'

'Well, I was never like those sados you see on the street, can of Special Brew in one hand, stinking of piss and accosting young girls for their loose change. I was never like that.'

'That's just semantics though. An alcoholic is an alcoholic however much money or class they may have. What is it that attracted you to drink in the first place?'

'Oh,' I said, slightly shocked at her bluntness. 'Well, I dunno really. I just liked the oblivion I suppose, I liked getting off my head, not caring about what I did.'

'Perhaps you could give me an example of something terrible that you did. Something that made you realise that alcohol was running your life.'

I looked about the place again and considered leaving. The thought even crossed my mind to find another pub where there were no troublesome councillors with shocking red hair forcing me to confess my sins.

'Why do you think that will help?' I said.

'It helps for us to face up to our problems, acknowledge what we're done and then take the consequences, face the music like a man.'

'Erum. Well I know the day that I realised it was the beginning of the end. The day that I realised I probably had a problem and that things couldn't go back to the way they were, and my actions had finally had a permanent affect.'

'Go on.'

'It was a normal evening really. Must have been about five years ago now. I was living not far from here, Fulham Palace road, in a house that my uncle had brought to rent out. Myself and three friends had needed somewhere to live so it had seemed like a good idea to move in there. I was celebrating as I'd just started a new job that very day, I'd been out of work for quite a while and so was pretty broke. However with my last £10 I decided to buy three bottles of wine instead of spending it on food or something sensible, like rent.

'Anyway we all settled down to watch a new series of Big Brother and I set to the drinking in a most studious manner. My mouth running away with me as it usually does. Now these three friends I meet just after finishing university and moving to London, back in those days we'd all worked in pubs and record stores and the only things we'd lived for had been pubbing, clubbing and drinking. Invariably matching each other bottle for bottle every night of the week. Was that something that just came with youth though, because as we grew older they all started to drink less and I more? Until it reached the point where it was just me that was drinking in the evening, every evening. They would wait for the weekends like most other people seemed to. It is a strange experience to realise that instead of counting the evenings that you *do* drink, you are counting the ones that you don't, which end up becoming few and far between.

'On this particular evening things descended further and further until I started spouting spiteful things at the three of them. 'Why do you have to drink so much, it turns you into a bastard?' my friend Johnny had asked at one point. 'Just to spite you,' I had answered, the venom behind my voice clear and obvious. Eventually I hadn't been able to put up with them having a go at me any longer so had gone out on my own to a club, not a penny to my name, I wish I could remember what on earth if did for drinks. Probably wandered round stealing other people's, or drinking leftover dregs, I just didn't care.

'Several hours and far too much booze later I'd returned to the house, where they were all now in bed, with two young girls who seemed to hang around in my local illegal off licence in tow, cackling and falling all over the place as we half fell and half staggered through the front door. It turned out, from talking to the owner of said shop a few days later, that I had offered them both a place to stay in my flat indefinitely if they so wished as long as they brought me some booze and came back to my flat to help me drink it.

'Each of my flatmates came and asked for us to keep the noise down at some point over the next few hours and all I'd done is yell abuse at each of them in turn, getting louder and louder as the night had gone on, being more and more offensive and abusive. I must have called them every name under the sun before I eventually passed out on the toilet, an empty bottle of vodka in one of my hands.

'The next day I'd woken to a huge hangover, unlike any I'd come across before or since and to an empty house. And when I say empty, I mean 'empty!' They'd taken everything. My flatmates were all in work and I was curled up round the u-bend of the toilet dead to the world. The two girls who'd come to stay must have seen their chance and taken everything, perhaps arranging for a friend to come round and help empty the place whilst it was void of life. It was actually pretty amazing that I had not woken up. How on earth they'd managed to get one of the sofas out of the door without making a sound or arousing suspicion amongst the neighbours was amazing. I just didn't understand it.

'When I'd finally met up with the guys on the Monday evening I had expected for them to come down on me like the proverbial ton of bricks, which they didn't. I'd expected rows and tantrums and for them to yell at me long and hard, for me to sit there and take it as I had always had to in the past. But strangely enough they remained quiet throughout, sitting high backed three abreast on the remaining sofa in the front room. They were grave and serious and it seemed more like a formal interview panel or disciplinary hearing for a repeat child offender by the school governors than four flatmates sitting around in their empty sitting room.

"Lucky they couldn't get that sofa out the door, eh,' I'd said, making a very ill-advised joke about our robbery, due to my bedroom being in the converted attic room I had been the only one who had got away from the robbery unscathed.

'We're going to move out,' said Johnny, clearly elected spokesman for the three of them.

'And that was all they said. Nothing more. A few more lines to let me know they were serious and how long it would be before they went, but apart from that they remained stony faced and silent throughout. Perhaps we could have gone on longer, but I couldn't take their looks or plain faced simplicity with how they were treating someone who was supposed to be their best friend. But then I suppose that was the point, they wouldn't have thought I would ever be able to act like that toward them, saying the things that I did, and inviting people into our house who would steal all their worldly possessions. It was merely my own medicine that they felt they were giving me, and boy did it hurt.'

The girl had drained her glass to half empty by the time I'd finished my story. I looked at my own glass to where the ice had now melted, the last few resilient pieces floating vacantly about in the brown, murky liquid. I had never wanted to drink it so much but also so little at the same time. It really was a paradox being an alcoholic. No matter what you go through, however many friends you lose or loved ones you hurt, no matter how many years you go without a drink, no matter what happens, if you sit down at a bar with a drink in front of you, a tiny piece of your brain will want to drink it. Some part of you will want that beautiful cloudy oblivion that only alcohol can bring. It is exactly why they say that once you are an alcoholic you will always be one, the best you can hope for will be to be a recovering alcoholic, which I now hoped I was.

'So what happened after that?' she said, sipping from her drink in what seemed like a provocative manner. Was she trying to cause a reaction in me? Or merely drinking her drink, the drink that she, as a non-alcoholic was more than entitled to have, after all she had not come to this bar to listen to me go on and on about my problems, but to have a quiet drink to help her relax on a Friday evening.

'Well, after that,' I went on, 'they all moved out, about two or three weeks later. And in way of adding injury to insult they refused to pay the final bills, leaving me with £600 to cover on my own, something I really did not need.'

'And what did you learn?'

'Not to invite girls into my house that steal all your things?'

'Anything else?'

'Don't trust Greek's bearing gifts?'

'Seriously.'

'Well why don't you tell me, you're supposed to be the professional?'

She sat back on her seat and took a good look at me. I suddenly became very self-conscious. She was not perhaps as plain as I may have thought when we first met. In fact, there was something about her eyes that drew me in. There was something there that let me know she was listening to me. I could see that she was feeling empathy just from her look, I felt comforted, like there was someone that understood me finally.

'What was the worst thing that you took away from the experience with your friends?'

'The worst thing? Probably the fact that I'd disappointed them, let them down one time too many and they just couldn't see any other way out of it than to leave me to myself. Let me drag my own way out of the pit I'd thrown myself into.'

'Did you hate them for abandoning you?'

'I think different processes work for different people. I quite easily could have used the rejection as a negative aspect and retreated further into myself, become even more of a drinker as so many people before me had. But instead I chose to use the kick up the arse they had chucked my way. I am not saying that I was cured that day, in fact it took several years after that. But that day was the beginning of the end. That was the day I realised that I had to stop hiding from myself and face up to the fact that I had a problem.'

'And what are you going to do now?'

'Now?'

'Yes, from now on, what are you going to do?'

'Well, much the same as I've been doing for the last three years probably. Try and tell myself what a bad idea it is to have a drink. The only thing is, it's so tiring. It's a constant pressure, a constant thing to think about, and something that has come to define me as a person. 'Hey you know that guy Pip?' 'Pip? No don't think I know him.' 'Yeah you do, the alchy!' 'Oh ye, the alchy, I know him."

'Yup, it'll be that. Tiring I mean. For the rest of your days probably. But remember that you're doing the right thing and you'll be fine. Keep your pecker up, as you English love to say.'

A pause hung between us. The song on the stereo came to an abrupt end and the general hub of conversation in the bar rose to compensate. I realised quite how much I had been speaking, my throat hurt. It felt like a great relief to be getting it all off my chest to someone who did not know me and could only form an opinion on what I said, and what I showed her.

'Can I ask you something?'

'What?'

'Are you really a councillor?'

'No,' she said, a coy smile spreading across her pretty mouth. 'I'm a primary school teacher. Which I suppose has elements of counselling involved with it. But then to be honest there doesn't really seem like there's that much to it, ask the right questions and let the person talk away.'

'I was thinking that maybe I could take you for a non-alcoholic drink some time?'

'Really?…well I'd love to but… I don't think my boyfriend would be too happy about that. It's one thing sitting in bars with boys and meeting accidentally, but going on an actual date, he might be a little funny about.'

'Boyfriend! Oh, sorry, didn't realise, I just assumed because…'

'…What? Because I'm sat in a bar on my own talking to you that I must be interested in you?'

'No of course not, I just… well… you know… where is he?'

'He's late. He's supposed to have met me here 20 mins ago. And lucky for you that he was.'

'If I ever have a child, you can teach it!'

'Well thank you very much,' she said, blushing slightly and sitting back to look about the place.

'What about your girlfriend then?' she said eventually. The music had been raised to an annoyingly audible din, Friday night slowly moving onto the next phase, I imagined in a few hours slow dances and hurried calls to flatmates to clean up any embarrassingly messy bedrooms in advance of regrettable one night stands.

'Ex-girlfriend.'

'Is there any chance of you two sorting it out then?'

'I don't think so. We'd been drifting apart for a while now, this break-up has been a long time coming and to be honest I just feel a little bit relieved. I think I've probably become a bit boring since I've stopped drinking.'

'I bet you haven't.'

'No it's ok, I don't mind. It's better than what I used to be like.'

I looked up at her, she was running her hand through her short hair again, ruffling it about until it lay in a more satisfactory, but very similar way. She smiled warmly at me.

'And what about your boyfriend, everything going well with him?'

She looked up, about to answer me, but then something over my shoulder grabbed her attention.

'Oh, there he is,' she said, waving her arm to attract his attention.

Suddenly a huge bouncer sized guy in a too tight suit

appeared at her side and into our little world. He grinned inanely at her and leaned low to kiss her on the cheek.

'David,' she said, 'I'd like you to meet…'

'Pip,' I jumped in, suddenly aware that I didn't know her name either. 'Nice to meet you.'

'Nice to meet you,' said the beefcake, who had a similar thick Nu Yook accent to the girl. 'Sorry I'm late honey, traffic was terrible.'

'That's ok. Pip here has been keeping me entertained. Shouldn't we be going?'

'Yeah, table's booked for 8, we're already pretty late. Pip, let me buy you a drink man, say thanks for keeping my girl company.'

He put his hand in his jacket pocket, ready to take his wallet out. I stopped him by raising my hand.

'No, that's fine. Thank you but I really don't want a drink.'

My eyes meet with the girl's and I noticed that her subtle smile was also now reflected in her eyes.

'It was a pleasure meeting you Pip,' she said, her hand outstretched. I shook it warmly.

'It was indeed,' I said. 'And thanks for the advice.'

She nodded and I glanced quickly at David who smiled down at me. I returned his smile rather awkwardly and then turned back to face the bar as they left. I noticed them holding hands as they ambled from the bar, clearly in no particular hurry to make their dinner arrangement.

'You done with that?' said the bartender, leaning somewhat distractedly over the bar and pointing at my still full glass of Jack Daniels, the ice now completely melted, a mere reminder of what had once been.

'Do you know,' I said, avoiding his stare. 'I think I probably am.'

AN ALTERNATIVE CANNES FILM FESTIVAL

'Will you stop playing with the bloody sand, Patrick,' snapped Alice.

Patrick, having not been aware he was playing with the sand stopped what he was doing. He looked down to see the project he had absentmindedly undertaken. A simple turreted sandcastle, formed from a discarded child's mould, sat in the midst of what had become a rather fancy set of fortifications. A moat, half on its way toward the sea to provide it with water ran the perimeter, which in turn gave way to a rising hillock on which the sand bailey sat amongst a set of shingle and seashell-based fence posts.

'Oh,' he said, sitting back on his haunches and wiping the sweat from his brow, unsure quite how this had come about. 'Hadn't really been…you know…' He trailed off and pulled himself lazily to his feet, stretching his back and squinting as he cast his gaze up and down the expanse of the midday packed beach.

'Patrick darling, must you try quite so hard to irritate me?'

'Sorry darling?'

'You are in my sun. Go and have a swim or something. Honestly you are acting just like a little boy.'

Ignoring his wife's advice Patrick sat himself back down on his purple beach towel, tapping the excess sand from his feet. His tall thin frame always felt uncomfortable on the beach, and as he lay down he found it too hot and immediately sat up again, drinking deeply from a bottle of warm water he had forgotten to put in the shade. He admired his castle network, idly wondering about extending the main section further south, toward the sea, but not quite finding the imputes to set to it.

'It's too damn hot,' he said, crossing his long legs, unsure what to do with himself. Remembering his sunglasses, he grabbed them from where they had been discarded on the floor and placed them on his peeling nose, flinching from the heat of the metal that had also been left out in the sun.

'Well go back inside then. It's the hottest time of the day. Why don't you go and have a beer or something.'

'You trying to get rid of me?' he asked, unable to hide the irritation in his voice.

Alice pulled herself up onto her elbows, her toned stomach muscles tightening as she moved. She wore a navy-blue bikini dotted with tiny white spots. Patrick could not help but think how good she looked, those six long weeks in the gym every day to build up for the annual Cannes trip had once again paid off. There was not an ounce of fat on her. The diet of nothing but cabbage soup helping see to that. He felt a twinge in his shorts but thought better of asking her to head back to the room for an hour or so.

'Don't be such a pratt, Patrick,' she said, wrinkling up her tiny nose and shaking her head dismissively as she looked at him. At least he thought she was looking at him, her huge Audrey Hepburn sunglasses meant she could have been looking anywhere. 'You are my husband, if I can't spend time with you then who the hell can I spend time with?' It was a rhetorical question, he hoped.

'Maybe next year we could try somewhere new.'

'What's wrong with Cannes?'

'Nothing, I just… well we've been here every year for seven years. Thought it might be nice to try somewhere… else… maybe just a different hotel. Just a thought, something we could consider...'

'Of course we can consider it, darling,' she said with a patronising smile, which meant they would not consider it at all. She lay back down and ran her hands up and down her long brown legs, annoying and arousing him in equal measures. He threw a towel over his lap and forced his glance back to the sea, looking without seeing at a small family playing in the break of the waves.

'Alright you two?' Nigel's shadow fell across the pair of them, the interruption bringing Patrick round from a sleep he had unwittingly fallen into. 'Nice castle, that you, Paddy?'

'Nigel, darling, please get the hell out of my sun. You're as bad as Patrick.'

'Oh, don't whinge sis, it doesn't become you. Makes you sound like nan.'

'And how many times have I asked you not to say nan, you were brought up better than that.'

Disorientated by sleep and the heat Patrick pulled himself up onto his elbows and tried to make out Nigel's shape, seeing only a brown black silhouette, great shards of golden light spilling out from behind him.

'Pat, Allie, I'd like you to meet someone, this is Rose.'

'Hello,' said a tiny voice Patrick could not make out the owner of.

'Hello, Rose,' said Alice's slightly cautious voice. 'You're a friend of Nigel's, are you?'

'We just met, in the sea, about ten minutes ago,' interjected Nigel, sitting on the end of Alice's towel, dripping water on her and forcing her to sit up. Patrick knew that her social decorum dictated she would not tell him off in front of a stranger, though he could see her desperate to.

'Turns out Rose here is quite the swimmer,' went on Nigel. 'She beat me hands down in a little race we just had. Swam for Great Britain, that what you said?'

'Well not quite Britain, England,' said Rose, placing herself carefully on the sand between Patrick and Alice's towels. She was a small, extremely pretty girl of maybe twenty-one or twenty-two. Her hair was so blonde it appeared platinum white in the midday sun. She had it tied back in a ponytail, resilient strands of which hung about her rounded face. Her body was toned and supple, but not as obviously so as Alice's, as if it had merely been a by-product of training, rather than the desired outcome. 'I swam the 200-metre freestyle for England when I was sixteen. Let myself slip in the last few years though, haven't been training nearly as much as I should have been.'

'Uni's been getting in the way eh, Rose,' said Nigel, rather crudely wringing out his long black hair onto the sand inches from Alice's shoes, Patrick wondered whether it was for Alice or Rose's benefit.

'Rose has just graduated from Cambridge studying Classics. Swimming and Classics, Pat, you hear that, you two should get on like a house on fire.'

Rose finally caught Patrick's eye and he matched her inquisitive look by reporting, 'I am a Classics teacher, at a private school in Kent, St. Sebastian's, do you know it?'

'Can't say I do. That must be very interesting.'

'He hates it,' said Alice, pulling herself up to sit cross legged, pocking her brother in the ribs as if the pair of them were sat as infants at the dinner table. 'Never stops complaining about the snobs and their money.'

'It's not all as bad as that. I also used to do a bit of swimming myself. In another life.'

'Oh, don't be so modest, Pat,' interrupted Nigel. 'He swam for his county when he was at school.'

'Yes, exactly, when I was at school, twenty years ago.'

'Do you still swim now?' asked Rose, her pretty blue eyes flicking over his face, taking in his features, he thought he wouldn't like the attention, he usually didn't, but something about this girl kept him at ease.

'I try to keep my eye in. Go about once a week or so. Not so easy what with the GCSEs and A-levels just gone.'

'We should have a race.'

'A race?'

'Yes. I'm afraid Nigel was not much competition.' Nigel frowned and looked rather hurt. 'Perhaps you could do better?'

'I doubt it very much,' said Patrick, looking first at a

disinterested Alice, and then a frowning Nigel, 'but I'm willing to give you a good run for your money.'

The day had reached its hottest part by the time they stood with the sea biting at their toes. Patrick turned to see Alice some thirty feet behind them, stretched out on her towel, vaguely fanning a fly from her face. Her brother lay on Patrick's towel, watching the pair of them intently as they stood.

'Your wife is very pretty,' said Rose, looking far out to sea.

'Yes, she is,' replied Patrick, unsure quite how to respond. 'She worked very hard on getting herself into shape for this holiday.

'She worked on getting herself ready to relax?'

'Seems bizarre doesn't it. She's the only person I've ever met who has a timetable for lying on the beach.'

'Have you been married long?'

'Almost eight years. She's the only person I've ever loved,' he said, as if it were the first time he had realised it, equally embarrassed for saying in front of someone he had just met.

'Right,' said Rose, stretching out her foot to test the water ahead of them. 'Shall we say out to that bathing platform?'

'The one with the man on it? That must be half a mile.'

'That a problem?'

'Of-course not. If that old fella can make it all the way out there I think I probably can.'

'Well then let's go. After three?'

After three they dove into the water, Patrick immediately trying to judge the pace and work out how quick she really was. The gentleman in him did not want to completely out swim her, but that same gentleman also did not want to be left embarrassingly in her wake. They battled on and it soon became apparent she was a much stronger swimmer than he, her sleek body cutting a fine waft through the water, barely breaking the surface she was so stream-lined, it was all he could do to keep up with her.

Every now and then he glanced up to see the bathing raft no nearer than the last time he looked, the looming presence of the fat man asleep on it a stark reminder of just how unfit he was. If that old guy could make it then surely he could. A hundred yards further and his muscles were starting to burn; Rose had pulled away from him now and was systematically baring down on the platform, one measured stroke after another. When he was still twenty feet away, she had reached it, she hauled herself up, leaping to a standing position with one jump. She stood laughing for a second, holding back her hair to drain some of the water, her chest heaving up and down with the exertion.

'Come on slow coach,' she called out to him. 'Get a move on, the sun is lovely!'

He pulled himself up onto the small platform, which was perhaps twenty feet squared. His arms stung from the unfamiliar exercise, and through heavy breaths he managed to say, 'No need to shout love, you'll wake the old fella.'

'Oh him, he's dead to the world, wouldn't worry about him.'

Patrick looked back to the beach and after a few moments managed to pick out Nigel's hunched form standing on the edge of the shore looking out at them, one hand to his forehead shielding his eyes from the sun.

'That's the furthest I've swum in years,' he said, his chest still not slowing. He could feel his heart beating fiercely against his ribcage, 'Wonder how on earth the old fella made it this far out.'

'Don't underestimate the elderly,' said Rose, walking purposefully over to the other side of the platform, careful not to slip over the side as it rose and fell as the waves passed underneath. 'My old granddad swam half a mile every Tuesday morning until he was ninety.'

'You know Nigel is stood watching us,' said Patrick, looking back to the shore. 'I think he might be quite keen on you.'

'I think you might be right.'

'And you don't like him?'

'I don't really like boys.'

'He is twenty-three. Older than you surely.'

'Well, that's as maybe. I've always been more attracted to men. Older men if possible. You know this old boy isn't moving. Do you think he's ok?'

Patrick pulled himself reluctantly to his feet, his legs sagging with his weight, and staggered across the uneven platform to where Rose stood leaning over the old man.

'Nigel just acts like a boy around Alice to wind her up, he knows she always rises to it, you know what it's like, you got any younger siblings?'

'No, only child. Should I wake him up?'

'Who Nigel? Oh, him. Yeah, probably should. He doesn't look very burnt, does he?'

'You alright mate?' she said, moving her hand to shake his shoulder ever so slightly. At her touch she withdrew her hand immediately, hugging it to herself. 'He's like ice,' she said.

Patrick leant down on his knees and touched the cool grey shoulder himself. He was freezing cold. The man, who must have been somewhere between fifty and sixty, lay with his mouth open and his eyes closed, just as if he were in a deep sleep. The longer they stared the more unanimated he seemed. He had a heavy-set build accompanied by a huge belly that protruded upwards despite the fact he was on his back. His jet-black hair was thin and receding and pulled back across his broad dome of a head. A thin moustache covered his top lip and seemed somewhat out of place. Patrick couldn't help staring at it, unsure what or even how to think.

'Is he breathing?' asked Rose, leaning low to kneel by Patrick's side. He managed to tear his view away and look her in the eye.

'I don't think so.'

'God,' said Rose, her hand covering her mouth.

Three hours later Rose sat on the back step of an ambulance shivering under a blanket despite the heat. Patrick, Nigel and Alice stood a few feet away, huddled in a small group against the throng of French officials that had swamped the beach.

'She doesn't look so good, does she,' said Alice, peering over Patrick's shoulder.

'No, she doesn't, poor girl. I should go and talk to her,' replied Patrick, making to move.

'No,' said Alice, a cold palm on his forearm. 'Let Nigel.'

At the mention of his name Nigel, who had been staring at the ground, looked up and with a moment's hesitation walked over to where Rose was sat. Patrick watched as he first tried to sit next to her, then changed his mind and laid a hand on her shoulder. She didn't seem to notice him.

'So they think he had been there all night then?' said Alice.

'Yeah. They're not sure but reckon he must have swum out sometime yesterday, then probably fell asleep and… well, didn't wake up.'

'Seems an awfully long way for someone his age to swim out to.'

'It does, yes. To be honest, I struggled, what with the undercurrent. But then he was hardly that old, fifty, maybe sixty.'

'Seems a strange place to put a bathing platform, so far out. Do they know who he is?'

'Don't think so. Had nothing on him but his swimming trunks. Strange that no-one missed him, if he's been there all night.'

'Plenty of people holiday on their own.'

'Do they?'

That night Patrick couldn't sleep. He lay in bed listening to the gentle sound of Alice's inconsistent breathing, a sound he had once found so endearing and comforting now seemed vaguely irritating. Had she always breathed so erratically before? She took a deep breath and then waited anytime between five and twenty seconds before breathing out. Eventually Patrick found himself trying to keep time with her, a practise he had always found helped him drift off in the past, but now only seemed to irritate him further. Instead, he tried to focus on the more consistent sound of the fan, but in the end his mind drew him back to the blank pale character on the bathing platform.

At about 3:30am the phone sounded its piercing shrill, shocking him out of the semi slumber he had fallen into.

'Hello?'

'Hi.'

'Rose? Are you ok?'

'Yeah… well… I… I don't really know. That man, I… I can't stop thinking about him… I… I can't sleep… do you think… maybe we could meet?'

Patrick looked over at Alice who lay on her front, locks of her usually immaculately kept hair lay across her face, one strand stuck to the side of her mouth where she had drawled.

'When?'

'Now.'

The beach was cold, the wind chill a severe contrast to the soaring heat from twelve hours previously, but there didn't seem anywhere else appropriate to meet. Rose was already there when he arrived, sat with that same blanket wrapped around her entire body, in the place where Patrick's towel had lain those hours earlier.

'It's so calm,' she said without looking up at him.

'The sea? Yeah. It's beautiful at this time of night. So

peaceful.' It seemed like the wrong thing to say but he couldn't think of anything else.

'So peaceful,' she repeated, pulling the blanket harder around herself.

'It's hard to believe there was a film festival on this very beach just a month ago.'

She remained silent, letting her eyes roll across the pitch-black horizon, perhaps looking for the bathing raft.

'Have you ever known anyone that died before?' asked Patrick, his voice low and careful.

'Only my father. When I was very little, five or six. I don't really remember him.'

'What did he die of?'

'He was an alcoholic. Nasty man by all accounts. One day, coming out of the pub at three in the afternoon, he stepped out in front of the 38 bus to Hackney Central. He was dead before he hit the ground.'

'I'm sorry. That must have been very hard for you… and your mother.'

'My mother was glad to be rid of him. He was more use dead than alive. Insurance paid for me to go to private school, where I learnt how to swim.'

'I s'pose what happened today has reminded you of that has it? Losing your father in such an unexpected way.'

'I tried to sleep but every time I closed my eyes there, he was. Lying like a beached whale on the platform. How did he get out there?'

'I'd been thinking that myself. He must have swum.'

'But why did no-one know he was there?'

'I don't know. I've been told to call the police tomorrow, they should have more information then.'

'Will you let me know?'

'Of-course.'

She turned her head and looked at him hard, he returned her look and smiled, which in turn caused her to smile, though seemingly against her will as she suddenly flicked her head back to the sea, the smile gone.

'I wish we hadn't had that stupid race,' she said, not turning back from the horizon, her long hair, now not tied up, fell about her shoulders, and caught by the wind whirled about her face like Patrick imagined a Banshee might look, she didn't seem to notice. 'If I hadn't forced you to swim out to that stupid bathing float thing then none of this would have happened.'

'None of what?'

She turned back to face him again, there were fresh streaks of tears on her cheeks, her hair was still caught in the wind, Patrick couldn't help but think of Medusa the Gorgon.

'We saw a dead body today Patrick. That might not mean a lot to you, but it does to me… I… he… he was so cold… like ice…' she trailed off and buried her head in a corner of the blanket.

'I'm sorry. I… I… that was insensitive. I've just… well I had a good friend die last year. It doesn't seem that strange to see another body now. I suppose it should really. No… it's not that it doesn't seem strange, it's just… when you've seen someone you know die, seeing a stranger dead isn't that bad. Not *as* bad. I'm sorry, look I'm saying the wrong thing, it must have been horrible for you.'

She looked his way again, her eyes red with tears. She smiled.

'Who have you seen die?' she asked, her voice tiny. Momentarily, he saw the six-year-old girl who had lost her father.

'A friend. A work colleague. My mentor. He died from lung cancer last year, I saw him fade from the biggest rugby playing giant you have ever seen to the saddest empty shell of a man.' An unexpected lump caught in his throat and he stopped talking, turning away to face the horizon himself.

'You know you can cry if you want.'

He gave a slight laugh. 'You know Alice has never said

that to me. Not in eight years of marriage. She sees crying as weakness.'

'Not weakness. Vulnerability.'

'She sees vulnerability as weakness.'

'It's not.'

He smiled at her, unsure what to say.

'Do you want a drink?' she asked.

A small silver hip flask appeared in her hand, she offered it out to him.

'What is it?'

'It helps. Trust me.'

He took it and drank deeply, the thick unfamiliar liqueur burning the back of his mouth and then his throat as he forced it down.

'What the hell is it!?' he managed between coughs, one hand rubbing his burning chest.

'I think I love you.'

'What?'

'And I think if you fucked me, it might go away. I might be able to escape from it. Might be able to sleep.'

'I'm not going to fuck you.'

'But your wife. You hate her.'

'I don't hate her. I love her very much.'

'I love you.'

'You don't even know me. We met this afternoon.'

'It feels like you're the only person that can understand.'

She unwrapped the blanket and stood, revelling her naked body. In the darkness her golden skin appeared as white as her hair had done in the sunlight. Goose pimples speckled her body and she shivered against the chill, a slight smile jutting up the corners of her mouth. A jolt of something: fear? lust? spread through him, starting in his loins but spreading through his belly.

'Do you like my body?'

'You are very… attractive…'

'You don't think my breasts too large?'

'... too... large...?'

'The girls at my swimming class used to mock me because of their size. They were all as flat as ironing boards, athletes tend to be, mine didn't seem to go away, no matter how hard I trained.'

'No. They're... very... very...'

'Will you sleep with me?'

He paused. It was only slight but then it was a pause none the less.

'No. I can't.'

She looked at the ground, crossing her arms over her breasts against the cold.

'Will you hold me then?'

He paused again.

'Of course.'

He picked up the blanket where she had left it and wrapped it round the pair of them, feeling her cool smooth naked flesh through his shirt. It felt good to hold her, she seemed to melt into his arms. He felt strong holding her. He hadn't felt strong in a long time.

The image of Alice in their bed flashed across his mind. What if she saw them? His marriage would be over. Good old dependable Alice, so reliable you could set your watch by her actions. Old familiar Alice, three years his senior, always telling him what to do and where to go. He didn't move but held the girl closer to him as she buried her head in the nook of his shoulder.

'I really don't think that was a very good idea, I feel dreadful.'

Patrick sat once more on the bathing platform, staring back at the neon beach front and blanket of blinking stars above. His chest was heaving so heavily he could hardly catch his breath. It felt like he was winded, it hadn't been like this before; every inch of his body seemed to ache.

'Look at the sky, such a number of stars. You can never see anything like this many in England. Grotty old

England!'

Rose, jumped and skipped round the platform like a little girl. 'Isn't it amazing out here at night, just amazing,' she continued, spinning around, her head held aloft toward the night sky.

'You've cheered up,' managed Patrick, his breathing still not slowing. Back on the beach they had both drifted off into a deep sleep before Patrick had come round to find Rose at the water's edge, still naked, down on her knees running her hands through the waves.

'Shall we swim out?' she had suggested. He immediately thought it a bad idea and told her, but she had persisted and as they had talked, she had grown more and more upset, less consolable and eventually forceful in her actions, shrugging off his attempts to calm her and pushing him away. Before long she had run headlong into the sea and started to swim, forcing him to follow her. Over halfway out she had stopped and floundered around before sinking below the surface, screaming for help. He had dived down and managed to drag her up and realising the platform was nearer than the land had been forced to continue out, swimming on his back and holding her under the chin, the way he had been taught at school, dragging her along in her semi-comatose state. As soon as he had forced her out of the water and onto the small wooden structure she had come alive and started her little charade of dancing and singing. He had been too tired to react, and now found that he just could not seem to calm down. His body convulsed, shifting uncontrollably before just as suddenly lying still, he could barely move, his arms and legs felt like lead weights.

'Let's get you out of those wet clothes,' she said, stopping her dance for a minute to pull off his sodden shirt over his head and fling it out into the sea. He was powerless to stop her and just about managed to lie on his back as she pulled off his shorts and threw them the same way as his shirt. When he was flat on the platform, she

climbed on top of him, took his head in her hands, he
could not have lifted it himself, and kissed him deeply. He
just about managed to react as she ate hungrily at him like
a lioness devouring her pray. It reminded him of kissing
teenage girls when at school, all passion and little
technique.

'What are you doing?' he spoke, but it wasn't him, he
didn't even recognise his own voice, where had it come
from, it felt distant and vague, far off, like an echo in the
night.

'Are you a breast or a leg man?' she asked, before
leaning forward and placing her left nipple in his mouth,
rubbing it hard over his lips whilst grinding herself against
him. 'I saw you staring at my tits on the beach.' Again, he
was unable to react and so just lay there as she ran her
breast round the outside and inside of his mouth and the
over his face, talking the whole time some insane
nonsense. 'Perhaps you'd prefer the wing, well… I haven't
got any of those… yet… ha ha ha…!'

'Rose,' the far-off voice said eventually. 'Rose. What…
what… are you doing…?'

'Rose? Who the hell is Rose,' she said, finally leaping to
her feet and pirouetting as she laughed, finding the whole
thing hilarious. 'My name is Tabatha, Tabbie… that's what
my dad used to call me anyway. He named me you see.
After he died, my mother couldn't face calling me that
name any longer so changed it to my middle name. Rose. I
think I prefer the sound of Tabbie, don't you?'

'Did… you…,' Patrick started, taking his time forcing
his words out. 'Did you… kill… that… man…?'

'Well done, Paddie! Can tell you're a teacher. Normally
they don't work it out until *after* I've fucked them. Poor old
sod yesterday, thought all his Christmases had come and
once when he found me crying on the beach, even
managed to get himself a little dingy to bring us all the way
out here, most useful for the return journey I must say. He
was the right size you see, the right build, too old though.

You on the other hand are just the right age.'

'For… what…?'

'For what?' she said, shaking her head at his ignorance, before leaning in close and whispering in his ear, 'For murder. You are the same age. Last night, he was the same size, perfect match. When I saw you on the beach it was just perfect, greying hair, pretentious style and feeling of self-righteousness, lording it over the other poor sods on the beach, like you and your fucking bitch of a wife owned the place. Shame I couldn't have topped her as well, but that isn't really playing by the rules is it.'

'The rules…?'

She carried on, ignoring him, 'And then that little prick of a brother-in-law started chatting to me, didn't realise it was going to be quite so easy…'

'You… are… mad…'

She leaned in low again, this time her face inches from his, the only part of him that didn't seem to have been affected by whatever she had given him, whatever had been in that hipflask, was his eyesight, and his hearing.

'That's as maybe mate, but… I… am… not… the… one… about… to… die…'

With one last kiss on the lips, she stepped out of sight. Patrick heard the sound of water breaking as she dived into the sea and then nothing, stillness, only the gentle lapping of the early morning waves on the abandoned bathing platform.

The next morning, at around 9am, Alice and Nigel stood arm in arm on the already heavily packed beach, life continuing around them, completely unaware of what had gone on those few hours before.

'Where do you think he's gone then?' said Nigel, shooing a stray fly from his face and drinking deeply from a chilled bottle of water, holding his head back and enjoying the sun.

'Don't know. And to be honest at the moment I don't

really care. He could be off fucking that stupid little girl, for all I know.'

'And he just disappeared in the night?'

'I woke at around five am and he wasn't there. God only knows where he's gone.'

'He has seemed rather strange these last couple of days.'

'He asked me yesterday about staying at a different hotel than here, about maybe not coming to Cannes next year.'

'Really? What on earth has got into him?'

'Oh, he's having some kind of sad mid-life crisis, well I'm not going to panda to it, and I'm certainly not going to go looking for him, if he wants to run away then that's just his own stupid problem.'

'He'll turn up eventually.'

'Not sure if I really want him to Nigel. I mean it's not the first time he's run away is it. Remember all that fuss when I had that silly meaningless thing with Geoff, he was gone for three days that time. Things have been going array for a while if I'm honest. I'm just not sure he's the man I met. And whatever happens I'm not going to let it ruin my holiday, come on, let's get down on the beach before all the good spots are gone.'

'Ok,' said Nigel, looking out to sea, suddenly catching sight of something. 'Oh look, that bathing raft from yesterday, looks like there's someone else on it.'

'Really? Silly fool that goes all the way out there after what happened.'

'True. Hey, fancy town later? Couple of margaritas, see where the night takes us?'

'Yeah, why not.'

CHEAP SHIRT

He was dressed in a cheap shirt. Like one I'd seen outside a shop on the Charing Cross Road: 3 for £10 the sign boldly declared. It was buttoned up to the top with no tie, a pet hate of mine. I didn't like him immediately.

'There's a place round the corner we could go,' he said, beady eyes flicking from side to side, cautiously watching others as they passed by. He could only have been 16 or 17; sporadic tufts of bum fluff covering his chin the only real sign of puberty having taken hold.

'A place?' I asked, intrigued by the type of establishments he may frequent.

'Yeah. There's this like low running wall, you can get down underneath and see who's coming, but they can't see you…'

'I know a place,' I said, lolloping my arm round his thin shoulders and steering him back down Charing Cross Road, further up from where I had seen those shirts.

The bar was called '79' and was populated with either small groups of gentlemen of my age and persuasion, or single gentlemen of my age and persuasion accompanied by younger gentlemen of the sort I had in tow. It was that sort of a place, dark and smoky – despite the new bad – people attempting to keep themselves to themselves.

'What can I get you…?' I asked, clinging to the bar and swinging round dramatically so I came face to face with the young chap.

'Carl,' he said, avoiding making eye contact. 'Should we not just… you know…'

'All in good time young Carl. All in good time. I like to buy my companions a couple of drinks first, to… relax the mood a little…'

'I have done this before you know,' he said hurriedly, his voice high and nasal, as if he was justifying losing his virginity to a group of sniggering school friends.

'I would expect nothing less,' I replied, laying my heavy hand on that same thin shoulder. He looked at it as if it was infected with a particularly nasty skin disease, but didn't flinch as I had expected him to. Not even the slightest little bit. 'Now, let me buy us a drink and then I'd like to hear a little bit about you.'

'Eh?'

'We don't say 'eh' darling, we say pardon.'

'Pardon?' he repeated, eyes scraping the sticky black floor.

I procured a bottle of white wine, not exactly a Bollinger, but then you pay for what you get don't you, and lead the way to a suitable corner, Carl flunking along behind me. The place was perhaps half empty, it being still earlyish on Saturday night. The plan was to get this boy done and then scoot over to Covent Garden for dinner with Graham and Martha in the Garrick, a lovely little French place opposite the club of same name. We sat down at a small table cloaked with a black tablecloth and covered in what appeared to be silver glitter. I relaxed, sighed and crossed my legs with a gentle click of my knee joints, smiling warmly and pouring the wine. Carl sat opposite me with his back to the rest of the bar, a position that clearly unnerved him as he checked over his shoulder every few seconds to see if anyone was watching us.

'This is where the Don would sit,' I said, sipping from my glass and attempting not to grimace too obviously against the taste.

'What?' replied Carl, confusion covering his vaguely pretty boyish features. I smiled again.

'The Don. The head of the mafia family. He would always find a table where he had clear sight of all exits and no-one could sneak up on him. It's a thing I have, every bar or pub I patronise I must find where the Don would sit. Learnt it from mother.'

A vacant sickly grin stole across Carl's face and as if seeing it for the first time he picked up the glass, sipping noisily, I couldn't help but think of the boys from the local park supping from their bottles of White Lightning and offering all sorts for another bottle, they could only be 12 or 13. The youth of today.

'So what do you do then Carl? College perhaps?'

He shook his head.

'No, thought not. Met a fella a couple of years older than you a few weeks back, putting himself through medical college. Imagine that eh. Drugs then I suppose, is it?'

He shook his head again and shrugged his shoulders. 'Nah, just need the money init.'

'Ah yes, the eternal cash flow need. Some people choose to work for a living, earning their simple crust via the grossly repetitive nature of the stoic daily grind; some lucky ones, myself included, have… how should I say… private forms of income to keep us in Bollie; and then there are other, rather curious creatures, who refuse to adopt either school and as such find themselves in all sorts of weird and wonderful worlds in an attempt to keep their heads' above water. They are, my young friend, my favourite sort.'

'Right.' He sipped again at his wine and half attempted that same slovenly grin before giving up and drinking some more wine, just as they all usually did.

'More wine?' I said, filling his glass, not waiting for a response.

'Cheers.'

'So. Is there anything you'd like to ask me?'

'Like what?'

'Well, like how much of this oh-so-precious-money I shall be imparting to you.'

'I told you the price.'

'Not much of a businessman are you boy. Surely you alter your prices depending upon social standing. You must have seen, or at least learnt in the short time we've been together that am either a rich man, or attempting to appear as a rich man, and as such either way you could hike your prices upwards to accommodate.'

'Oh right. Yeah, well, in that case the price has gone up to 100.'

'That's far too much, I'm afraid. Couldn't possibly afford that.'

'But you…'

'I'm joking my young cherub. I actually have something much more idyllic in mind. Ever been to the Ritz?'

'No.'

'Would you like to.'

He took a furtive glance at his watch. 'Got football in an hour.'

'Well, you certainly know how to douse the flames don't you. You wouldn't like to stay in a 5-star room for the night drinking real wine and ordering whatever takes your fancy from room service?'

'And getting paid?'

'Indeed.'

'How much?'

'Well, I assumed your rate was by the hour.'

'It… er… is…'

'So, do we have a deal?' I uncurled my long bony fingers and extended my hand across the table in an attempt to seal the deal. I had always hated the sight of my skeletal hands and only took to using them when I really had to.

He paused for a second, looking at my ugly hand. Was it putting him off? Surely that would be a first. 'His hands are so awful, even whores won't sleep with him.'

'I don't know.'

'You don't know what?'

''bout staying at the Ritz and that. I mean… I would well like to but… well football, it's the quarter finals and we've got a well good chance of winning against these fuckers… I mean… thanks for the offer and that but… well you know.'

'I see.'

To say my sails were deflated was a tad of an understatement.

'Fifty then, is it?' I asked, digging out my wallet from my inside jacket pocket.

'That's right. You want me to do it right here?'

'I most certainly do. Let's get it done shall we. Under you go, son.'

Without further hesitation his head sank beneath the table and I felt the familiar sensation of my fly being unzipped. Only in London, I thought to myself, sighing and taking another sip of the vile wine. Only in London.

THE CURSE OF AULUS PLAUTIUS (A HORROR STORY)

In the dimly lit kitchen of number 15 Borderdale Street, Homerton, East London, Rosie the housekeeper's hands shook as she lifted the too heavy kettle once more from the huge open fire. She placed it on the old oak table and sighed with relief, wiping her forehead and cursing the master yet again for refusing to get any electric appliances in the house. This was the 21st Century, she told herself, it felt like they were stuck in the dark ages. Nothing had been updated since his parents had died almost 50 years before, which was all well and fine for him, sat in his library all day long, his long thin nose scraping away at one history book after another, but she had to do all the cooking and cleaning, which at her age was becoming more and more difficult.

He was so superstitious, wouldn't even get out of bed if there was one magpie on his windowsill in the morning; terrified of technology, and he probably thought, but hadn't said as much, that by keeping the house in the same state it would keep evil spirits at rest. Nonsense. Him and his damn spirits.

The window rattled yet again and drew Rosie's attention from the steaming pot of tea she was preparing. It was certainly going to be some night out there; the rain hadn't started yet but wasn't far off. A thick ray of silver light flicked suddenly over the windowpane, a shiver ran down her spine and she pulled her shawl about her. She hadn't seen anything like that since… well for a long time. She shook the memory from her head and turned her attention back to the teapot. If she was going to get home before the rain started, she'd have to be quick with dinner.

Upstairs in the master bedroom in his huge four-poster bed old Tom Wimpole coughed heavily as the dust from the huge history volume he was holding tickled his throat. He reached for the glass of water on the bedside table without taking his eyes from the volume, he was nearly there, surely this must be the book, he had read every other one. His fingers failed to clasp the vessel and instead sent it over the edge of the table where it landed with a thud on the thick shag pile carpet. Cursing, he lifted the blankets back and climbed from the bed, leaning low to pick it up. As he did a beam of silver light glanced across the far wall and caught his eye. What was that? The glass forgotten he shuffled over the floorboards in his pyjamas to the window that looked out on the huge over-grown back garden. The garden he hadn't been in for almost 50 years.

The wind rattled the tall ancient trees that stood almost as tall as the house, flailing their long leafless branches from side to side as if they were men possessed. Where was that beam of light? His eyes were old, but a lifetime spent reading books and digging for details had kept them sharp. The murky blackness gave nothing away. Perhaps he had been wrong. He checked his watch. 14th November. Still three months to go. He must have been mistaken. Silly old fool, seeing things now. He turned to head back to bed and as he did he caught that same glint of silver light from the corner of his eye. He scanned the garden again and then saw it. As clear as day. Just as he had all that time ago. It was starting already. He was routed to the spot. Frozen with terror. He thought he'd noticed an odd feeling in the air the last few weeks. Strange things were starting to happen again. Were those dogs wailing he had heard the other night…?

He forced himself from the window, turning his bulky weight and heading for the chair where he'd flung his clothes an hour before. There was so much to do. So many preparations to be made. Three months was not a long time at all.

As he reached for his shirt with a shaking hand, a tingle

ran down his left arm. Not a time to be feeling ill. He shook it to clear the feeling, but it wouldn't go. It intensified into a sharp pain. Suddenly the pain had moved to the middle of his chest. It was like he was being stabbed. He was having a heart attack. Not now. Not now!! So much to do.

At that moment the door swung open, and Rosie appeared, preceded by her huge wooden tray cluttered with various dinner things. She saw Tom lying by his bed and in her surprise dropped the tray on the floor with a huge clattering bang, she ran to his side.

'Master? What happened?'

Tom found he couldn't talk. The pain was so intense he couldn't focus. Rosie helped him back to the bed and he lay down, the pain briefly abating enough for him to speak.

'Paper,' he said, clutching at his chest as the pain intensified again. 'Pen and paper. Envelope.'

Open mouthed Rosie nodded and made for the door. He watched her go. Would she be able to help? He suspected not. He suspected it would only be a certain type of person that would be able to end what he put into motion those 50 years before. She was bound to read what he wrote though, she wouldn't understand, not her, he would have to write in code, guide whoever finds the letter to work out what needed to be done. They would only have three months. The pain stabbed again, worse than ever, and he buckled over, gritting his teeth hard against the spasm. He knew he didn't have much longer left. Where was Rosie with that damn paper?! He needed to write his last wishes, a guidance, a warning even, before this attack got him for good.

-

Just over two months later, after the frivolity of Christmas and New Year had finally abated and the cold weather, so comforting and easily ignored over the holiday season, had turned into the bitter chill of the New Year grind, Hackney lay as it always did at the time of year. No longer did families watch from behind whitened windows at the beauty of the frost and snow that covered the roads and pavements, the frost lay thicker, darker and more dangerous and the snow had become an ugly grey/black sludge. People trudged from place to place as little as possible, eyes glued to their path, teeth gritted against the cold and chins pushed deep into scarves and collars, hiding from the biting wind.

Through this milieu a little blue Honda Civic unfamiliar to the area found its way, turning the last lazy corner onto Borderdale Street and skidding to a halt outside the huge Victorian House of Number 15. The engine chugged once more, launched the car a foot further forwards and then died. Across the road a streetlamp blinked into life, casting its dull neon glow over the pavement, the tip of which didn't quite reach the front step of the house. It was 3.30pm.

A figure emerged from the car and clapping his hands against the cold ran to the boot, covering himself in a thick black puffer jacket.

'Come on everyone,' he called into the car. 'We've made it! Grab what you need, the delivery van won't be here 'til tomorrow morning, we'll have to rough it tonight.'

Three more figures clambered reluctantly from the car and took their places on the pavement next to him, the whole family looked up at the dark building, not even an inch of light seemed to reside behind any of the inky black windows.

'Looks different… eerie,' said Nick, the 14-year-old son.

'That's because it's dark,' replied his father, Nigel, taking the woman, Karen, by the waist and leading her up the path. The little girl, Kerry, followed along behind her mother leaving just Nick left on the pavement, shivering against the chill. Suddenly aware of another presence he spun round to see a black dog sitting across the road staring back at him. It sat stock still, not even wagging its tail, the occasional blink of its coal black eyes the only sign of life. Nick watched it for a second and then turned and headed up the path after his family.

The next morning Nick woke with a start. He was alone on the floor of an empty room. It was silent. So silent he could hardly bear it. This must be his new room. He could just about remember falling through the door late the night before. The walls were thick and covered in chipped white paint, the high ceiling sporting looped curls of the same white paint also chipping at the edges. He climbed out of his sleeping bag, noting how cold his nose and ears were and crossed the vacant floorboards to the large bay window that looked out into the garden beyond. It was overgrown. Looked like it hadn't been cared for in years. Green and brown leafless trees with long wicker like branches stuck out from the thick undergrowth of bushes, brambles and grasses that seemed to cover every other inch of the garden. On the far wall sat a black cat staring straight back at the house. Its long tail swooping casually back and forth behind it. A shiver ran down his spine. What a place. He sighed and thought about his old home. Just two days ago they had been in South Wales in comfortable Swansea he knew so well. This place wasn't right. He could feel the weight of the years on his young shoulders. He wanted to go home. He missed his mother and he wanted to go home.

In the kitchen his father sat at the table whilst his stepmother fanned pointlessly at the huge open fire. Kerry sat in her highchair playing with a bowl of porridge.

'Why is it so damn cold, dad?' said Nick, pulling up a seat at the table and taking a piece of cold toast from the wrack, he bit into it without adding butter or jam.

'Central heating's on the blink. Don't worry, we've got

heaters coming with the van, should be here any minute…'

'… Nigel, help please…!'

Nigel darted up and grabbed Karen by her waist just before she keeled over. He took the huge tin kettle from her hands and placed it on the table, laughing. Together they seemed an odd pair, her all legs, high heels and hips with long jet-black hair she usually had tied in a lazy ponytail high on her head, if he had to guess Nick would have put her at 32. His father was taller and thicker set and in his mid-40s, a lifetime spent on building sites and rugby pitches gave him a slight oafish demeanour.

'Butter fingers! Watch out or you'll ruin our lovely new floor.'

'The floor's about a thousand years old, more importantly, why on earth are there no electrical appliances in the kitchen? Or anywhere for that matter. The estate agent said this place came fully furnished, family wanted a quick sale,' said Karen moving back over to the table, righting her meticulous black shirt, she was the type of woman who never had a speck of dust on her.

'Dunno. Old fella who lived here was some kind of recluse apparently, afraid of technology or something,' replied Nigel taking his wife by the waist and pulling her close. 'I reckon he just wanted to make more work for the women.'

'You sexiest pig,' said Karen, slapping him playfully on the chest. They laughed together and then embraced, Nigel kissing his young wife deeply. Nick looked away and shook his head, taking another bite of the cold dry toast.

'Dad,' he said, his head still turned away. Nigel didn't respond. 'Dad! Dad!'

'Yes! What is it, Nicholas?'

'I asked you not to call me that.'

'Sorry… Nick. What is it, Nick?'

'Are we still going to see mum's grave tomorrow?'

Nigel looked at Karen who walked immediately away to lean on the counter. She caught his eye and gave him a stark loaded look.

'Oh sport,' began Nigel, pulling himself onto the chair next to Nick. 'I'd forgotten all about that…'

'Well I hadn't. It'll be four years tomorrow. Four years, dad.'

'I know. I know son, I was there. I'm hardly going to forget it am I? It's just, well I promised Karen we'd pick her grandmother up from the station, she's going to come and stay with us for a few days. She grew up round here, wanted to see how the area has turned out.'

'We've only just moved in.'

'I know, but,' he took a glance over at Karen, who had buried her head in a magazine. 'Well I promised Karen.'

'Dad! You promised me!'

'Don't shout at me Nicholas!' Nigel sprang to his feet, suddenly angry. He slammed his fist onto the table. He was an imposing figure when angry. Nick had always been scared of him. Little Kerry stopped eating and started to cry. Karen tutted and moved across to pick her up.

'Look what you've done now,' she said, making shushing noises as she moved the toddler from side to side, she left the room, giving Nigel a look over her shoulder as she did.

'Listen Nicholas. I know you miss your mother, but… but we've all gotta move on, this is a new start for all of us.'

Nick remained silent, he knew there was little point in arguing.

'Listen,' repeated his father, sitting down again and rubbing the top of this head. 'We'll find another time to go and see your mother. Ok son? I want to go too. I promise. Ok?'

'Ok,' said Nick, unable to make eye contact. 'S'pose I could go out and try and explore the area a bit.'

'Well, that's another thing,' said his father, standing up and moving round the other side of the table. 'Karen… both of us… were kind of hoping you might babysit Kerry for us.'

'Oh, dad.'

The next afternoon and apart from his stepsister, who seemed content in front of a farmyard DVD, Nick found himself alone in the huge Victorian house. Despite the busy little community that Homerton seemed to provide he could not help but notice how quiet it was. When you were in the kitchen, which lay at the back of the house, you could almost imagine you were in another world it was so silent.

He wandered aimlessly from room to room finding nothing out of the ordinary apart from one room at the very top of the second floor that had a looked door. He tried to turn the huge cast iron handle, but it would not move. Back downstairs he checked that Kerry was still suitably occupied and then headed into the kitchen where another huge iron cast door marked the entrance to the garden. The walls were 15 feet high on either side and there didn't seem to be another gate so as far as he could work out this was the only entrance. The huge bolts were stiff and had long ago been painted down but with a bit of vigour he managed to free them and pull the great door on a wide arc toward him. It creaked ominously as it went but provided little resistance, which seemed strange considering how long it had been shut and the sheer size of it. Putting the thought to one side he stepped over the threshold.

It was hard going but slowly and surely, he made his way forward, huge green brambles and nettles sweeping at his jeans as he pushed on. The garden was not huge, but it gave the impression of being a lost world, like a jungle, and the further he pushed on the more a part of that world he became. At one point he slipped as a bramble found its way taught round his ankle and as he turned the house veered without warning back into view, sending a wave of shock rushing through him. It was so huge and imposing and seemed suddenly out of place. The back of the house was even darker and more sinister than the front, the walls charcoal black and the dark windows reflecting the winding branches of the barren trees he was amongst.

He caught his breath and turned once again, choosing to head into the far top hand corner of the garden, where the brambles seemed not so high. He found out the reason they seemed shorter with his next few steps, the ground suddenly slopped downwards, the garden continuing round a corner out of sight of the house. The change in gradient caught him off guard and before he could stop himself he had toppled forwards, landing with a jolt of pain on his shoulder and slipping down the steep slope. He grabbed fistfuls of plants, but they just tore free from the ground and suddenly he was on his front, falling head over heels, crashing through the undergrowth, brambles wiping and stinging his face as he went.

Landing with a thump on his head he was immediately disorientated, and it took a few seconds for the world to come back into focus. He looked at his hands which were sore and swollen from where he had grabbed nettles and brambles alike. There were a few grazes and cuts on his legs and what felt like a nasty gash above his eye but apart from that he seemed unhurt. Letting himself catch his breath he slowly started to calm down, looking about and finally seeing where he was. He stood but the undergrowth was taller than him and he could not make out where he was in relation to the house. He took a hesitant couple of steps forward and his foot hit solid rock. Moving the vegetation aside he saw it was some kind of huge stone table, sat next to the wall but made of different brick. It was covered in strange carvings and seemed to be carefully sculpted. It must have been hundreds of years old. What on earth was it doing at the bottom of this pit in his garden? Perhaps it was valuable. Had he just uncovered some ancient artefact? Maybe he would be famous!

Moving more of the brambles and grasses aside he

finally made out the dimensions. It was about six feet wide
and four feet deep and slightly buried in the ground so
impossible to tell how high. Perhaps this was only the tip
of what it could be. Perhaps it was a whole building he had
found. He ran his bloated fingers over the weird circles
and spheres that covered the top and sides. Such strange
markings. What did they mean? The very top seemed to be
a slab about eight inches thick. Was it the cover? Was this
a box of some kind? His injuries now ignored he placed a
hand on either side and heaved as hard as he could.
Nothing happened. It didn't move an inch. He tried again.
Looking around he found a thick wooden stick discarded
some way off. Using this as a lever he managed through
shear desperation to haul the cover a few inches free. An
ancient sigh escaped as the stale air from inside hissed out
into the world. Nick coughed as he breathed in the dust
and nearly dropped his lever, just managing to prevent it
from falling at the last second.

Everything fell silent.

He was aware of a complete lack of noise. No sound of
the birds in the air or wind in the branches. Complete
silence. The light seemed to change. Ever so slightly,
almost unnoticeable, just as if a heavy cloud had moved in
front of the sun on a clear day it grew darker. Nick looked
about him, but nothing seemed to be happening, as if the
world was frozen in time. Slowly he became aware of a
deep throbbing noise coming from inside the stone box he
stood in front of. It grew louder and louder until a sudden
burst of noise was followed by a flash of silver light. Nick
froze but nothing more happened. With the flash of light
the world seemed to return to normal. He could even hear
the faint sound of birds chirping in the distance.

He looked himself over but nothing out of the ordinary
seemed to have happened to him. What was the weird
silver light? And that throbbing noise that swelled from
nowhere? The hairs on the back of his neck stood on end
and he realised for the first time how scared he was, he

looked at his hands, they were shaking, but despite this he couldn't move away. The stone box covered with strange markings seemed to draw him in. He moved closer. Without making a conscious decision to do so he grabbed the stone lid where he had wrenched it free and lifted it up. It lifted much easier than before. He had to see what was inside. He had to know. The higher he lifted it the more light from above fell in, the shadows slowly retreating across the space. Before long he held the lid directly up and peered into the murky darkness, trying to prepare himself for what he might see.

Inside there was a body. A skeletal body, covered in leather binds from head to toe. One long grey arm pushed out from the binds and was held out away from the body, as if it was trying to escape. The bottom jaw fell away from the top, giving the impression it was screaming. Or had been screaming. A wash of terror flooded through him. What had happened to this person? What had the silver light been? His soul escaping? He could barely allow himself to think of the possibilities.

He lowered the top and took a step backwards, noticing how the shaking had spread from his hands to his legs as well. He could barely stand. He had to get back inside.

Back in the kitchen he sat at the table and placed his heavy head in his hands, breathing deep and trying to think about the enormity of what he had seen. A body in a stone box at the bottom of his garden. Not your everyday occurrence. What should he do now? Tell his father? Call the Police?

Before he could do anything there was a sound from the living room. Kerry! He had been so wrapped up with searching the garden he had forgotten all about her. He raced into the lounge to find her climbing over the grate of the huge iron cast fireplace. Her head obscured by the chimney.

'Kerry!' he screamed, launching himself across the room and grabbing at her. She looked at him, startled by his sudden appearance, and then seconds later broke into a wail of tears. He lifted her up and tried to make placating quieting noises.

'Look at you,' he said, setting her down in the middle of the room. 'You are covered in soot, what is your mum going to say?'

Eventually she calmed and after he had tickled her, she even started to laugh, her little face the picture of childhood innocence once more. She picked up her rattle and thumped it up and down on the rug, smiling and giggling, gurgling noises escaping her mouth. He moved over to check nothing had changed with the fireplace, and just before he moved back away, satisfied nothing had been altered, something caught his eye. He bent down and picked up a small white rectangle from the middle of the fireplace. It was a letter. Kerry must have dislodged it in her scramble.

'Strange place for a letter eh Kerry,' he said, opening the seal and pulling out the thick wad of paper and a large plain black key. He looked the key over and put it in his pocket. 'They can't have used that fire much.'

The letter consisted of five thick off-white pages and appeared to be in some foreign language, the long looping letters ornately swooping over the pages. He recognised one of the words on the first line. Tempus. Tempus, Latin for time. The letter must be written in Latin. Had it not been for his experience in the garden only a few minutes before he may have found discovering a letter in the fireplace rather weird, but he was certain that nothing would seem strange ever again. He sat down and tried to translate it but could not get very far. He had been dreadful at Latin and had given it up as soon as he could. His friend Martin back in Wales would be able to though. Perhaps it had something to do with the body in the garden. He would send it to Martin and ask him to translate. Give him a good excuse to get in contact as well. Should he tell him about the body? Probably best not to at the moment. It would be best if he told his dad and then let him decide what to do. He looked out of the window into the overgrown garden once more. The whole experience already seemed distant and far away, like a dream he had had long ago. Almost as if it hadn't happened at all.

'I mean, there's a lot of work to be done, sure… but… but well I didn't spend 20 years on the sites in Swansea for nothing now did I… I relish the challenge… we relish the challenge, don't we love…' Nigel was speaking to Karen's grandmother, a tiny grey haired old lady called Maud who Nick didn't think looked a thing like Karen. The grandmother sipped quietly at her soup.

'That's nice,' she said with a gentle smile.

'Nigel, do you think anything's wrong with Kerry?' asked Karen from the other end of the table. Nick looked up, hoping her trip in the fireplace hadn't done her any harm, she had been fine when he had helped her out, but had seemed much quieter as the day had worn on.

'No. Why? She got a temperature?'

'No, nothing like that, she just seems so… well quiet I suppose.'

'Thought you'd love a bit of peace,' replied Nigel, leaning back in his chair and laughing to himself.

'Dad. I went in the garden this afternoon.'

'Yeah? Bit rough init. Could do with a clear out. Pass the potatoes will you son.'

'I… I fell down a slope, and… well I found something. I don't think you'll believe this…'

'Yeah? A slope eh. What did you find?'

'I found a stone box, must be ancient, and inside… inside there was a body.'

'A body? What type of a body?'

'Well, a skeleton. But it was definitely a body. There

was this weird thumping sound and then this flashing light and everything went silent…'

'You found a skeleton in a box in the garden? Our garden?'

'Well… yeah. There was this weird light and…'

'People don't bury other people in gardens, son. Probably a dog or something like that. People bury their dogs in the garden all the time. I'll take a look tomorrow.'

'Do you not think we should maybe call the police or something?'

'I said I'd take a look tomorrow. Not worrying the police with a dog's skeleton on a Sunday night…'

'But dad…'

At that moment Karen stood and picked Kerry up out of her highchair, her own chair causing a long drawn-out creak as it scratched the stone floor.

'I'm taking her to bed,' she said, moving toward the door. 'I'm not sure about her at all. She's probably over tired or something. She's just normally such a happy child.'

Nigel let her go and then turned back to lean his huge elbows on the table.

'So Maud,' he said. 'You used to live round here then. What's it like coming back after all this time?'

'Strange indeed,' said Maud, putting down her soup spoon and sitting up straight in her seat, her shoulders only just visible over the top of the huge table. 'I was billeted away from here during the war. 1940, I think that was. The Nazi's dropped bombs all over this area, whole of London was nearly destroyed. Different place back then. A bomb came down in this very back garden, you know. Missed the house by feet. Probably explain the slope you fell down earlier, Nick.'

'Did you know the people that lived in this house before?' asked Nick, leaning forward, suddenly interested in the conversation.

'Certainly did. They kept themselves to themselves mostly. After the war I came back and folk said they had become even more reclusive. Said strange things started to happen.'

'Strange things,' asked Nick. 'Like what?'

'Nothing much really. Things going missing. Sounds in the night. Screams coming from the house. That sort of thing. People never used to let their animals go too near as it sent them mad. Couple of pets turned up dead once or twice.'

'There you go Nick,' Nigel interjected. 'There's your dead dog. Must have been buried in the garden. People probably had a big dog of their own. Fought all the others and killed 'em.'

Maud looked slowly over at Nigel, who was now sitting back in his chair, but didn't seem annoyed by his interruption. She turned back to look Nick in the eye.

'Then one day, quite a few years later, the whole family save for the boy disappeared. No-one knows where they went. Some said they went mad and died and others that the son had killed them all, but either way no-one ever found out for sure. Still don't know to this day.'

'And what happened to the boy?'

'He stayed here. On his own. Looked after by a housekeeper for the next 50 years. Must have been him that died just recently. He had no more family to leave the house to, so it went up for sale.'

'Strange,' said Nick, after the story had hung in the air for a second. 'So the whole family just disappeared?'

'That's right. Father, mother and two girls. No-one knows what happened to them.'

'Nonsense,' cut in Nigel again. 'Someone must know. Stories just get taller over time. They probably all fell ill and died together. People always need to make up a story about it don't they. Boy survived and stayed on. Are you suggesting it's some kind of curse?'

'I'm not suggesting anything Nigel. I just know what I heard at the time.'

With the hint of a smile on her lips Maud looked from

father to son and then picked up her soup spoon again.

That night Nick slept badly. He finally had his things about him, even his old bed, but still something didn't feel right. He dropped off past 1am into a fitful sleep filled with dreams of flashing silver lights and a leather binding reaching up from a stone box and winding its way round the whole house, slowly strangling it until the walls caved in and it was crushed into a tiny shape and dragged into the deep of the dark stone coffin at the bottom of the garden.

He woke with a start. Unsure where he was. It was pitch black, his desk clock said 3.04am. Outside a storm raged. From where he lay, he could just make out those same madman's arm branches as they were swung relentlessly from side to side. A bolt of lightning was immediately followed by a clap of thunder, both startled him.

Turning away from the window onto his side he stared across the room. The shadows danced creepily over the walls as the curtains swayed in time with the storm. The pale moonlight peeking in when the curtains fell the right way.

The door moved.

At first he thought it must be a trick of the light, or just the wind as it was not shut but pushed against the frame, but soon it became clear that the door was being slowly opened from the outside. Someone, or something, was trying to get in.

He watched, frozen with terror, unable to move his body or his eyes away from the movement. When it reached almost a foot wide a tiny shadow fell across the floor and a figure emerged into view.

It was Kerry.

Nick breathed a sigh of relief and sat up in his bed, swinging his legs over the side.

'Kerry,' he said, holding his hands out to her. 'Are you

scared of the storm? Don't worry, come to Nicky, I'll take you back to bed.'

She moved forward into the room. Something wasn't right. She wasn't walking with her usual toddler stumble, and there were no gurgling noises or sounds of any kind. The curtains blew suddenly to one side and a beam of moonlight fell across the room catching Kerry in its wake. She didn't look like herself. Her face was frozen in one gloomy expression and her eyes were wide and… silver. Her eyes were silver and her face had a glazed look to it. As if she was made of wax. Terror coursed through Nick's body. He stood but stumbled on the edge of the rug and landed with a thump on his front. Kerry moved forward until she was just above him and raising one of her tiny arms seemed like she was about to hit him. He rolled onto his side and she held the arm in place, moving round to compensate.

'Kerry, what are you doing?' said a voice that sounded like his own. 'Kerry, stop!'

He rolled out of the way again, narrowly avoiding her advance, leaping to his feet and throwing himself across the room. Surely a three-year-old couldn't hurt him? So why was he so scared?

'Kerry?' he said again from the other side of the room, she turned and proceeded his way, both arms now outstretched in front of her, that mad silver glow in her eyes. 'Stop!' he yelled as loud as he could, outside another flash of lightening threw an arc of light across the room. 'Help! Help!'

He crossed the room and Kerry continued her advance, reaching out for her. She made to grab him, and he held her in place. She had surprising strength for a child and managed to wrench her arm free, again trying to hit him, he moved his own arm up to shield the blow and caught her a glance across the forehead, sending her flying backwards onto the floor. She landed with a thump and banged her head behind her on the floor.

'Kerry!' he cried, rushing forward to grab her in his arms. Her expression had not changed at all. At that moment the door flung open, and his dad and Karen appeared in the room.

'What the hell is going on…?' said his father, hitting the light switch, momentarily blinding Nick.

'It's Kerry,' he said, 'she's gone mad.' He looked down at the girl who also seemed to have been stunned by the light. She was not crying from where she had knocked her head.

'She must have been sleep walking,' said Karen, kneeling and taking her daughter from Nick's arms.

'She wasn't sleep walking, she was… she was possessed…' started Nick but neither of them was listening to him. Nigel had picked Kerry out of Karen's hands and was making to leave the room, Karen followed; she stopped at the door and almost as an afterthought turned to face Nick.

'Are you ok?' she asked, and did at least look concerned.

'I'm fine. Is she? She tried to attack me.'

'Sleepwalkers do strange thing.'

'Has she slept walked before?'

'I don't think so. She's not at all well though. I'm going to take her to the hospital in the morning. Try and get some sleep. See you in the morning.'

Nick snorted a laugh. 'Yeah right,' he said.

The next day, whilst his father and stepmother were with Kerry at the hospital Nick found himself sat at the table, that extreme silence that the house seemed to be seeped in once again hanging over the kitchen. Despite knowing it was set deep in London he just couldn't help but think of the house as being in the midst of a wilderness. As if to iterate his thoughts branches scrapped along the window breaking him from his concentration. He thought of the body. Because of the fall his head had been swimming at the time. Had he really seen it? Perhaps his dad was right, maybe it was just a dog in its grave and his confused mind had embellished the rest.

He thought about Kerry the night before. She had been possessed. It seemed like too much of a coincidence for him to find the body, see that strange silver light escape at the same time, and then for Kerry to go mad that same night. It must be connected. But what was it all about? As farfetched as it all seemed it must be connected. The letter was the final piece of the jigsaw. He needed to know what it said. With any luck Martin would get back to him soon.

Not wishing to go back out into the garden just yet he wandered around the house again, stepping in and out of rooms at random and ending up on the second floor once more stood outside the locked door, the only room he hadn't yet been inside. A thought occurred to him and he pulled out the key he had found the day before. It fit the lock perfectly and after a bit of force it turned and the old door creaked open.

It was a library. Filled with shelf after shelf of books, as high as the ceiling and running the length of the building all the way to the back wall where a window looked out on that same garden. A huge old oak table sat in the middle of the room covered in papers and books seemingly pilled at random. He wandered around and leafed through them but found nothing of real interest. A thick layer of dust covered everything.

Whoever had written the letter had planned for the person that found it to come into this room. Did this have anything to do with the body in the garden? There must be something in the library that he was supposed to find. But what? A book? But it could be any of them. There were hundreds. He wandered up and down for a while looking in vain at random titles, and then eventually found himself stood at the far window looking down on the garden far below. From this top storey he could almost make out the area where the stone box was, could almost see round the corner of the wall, but not quite. It really was like another world. What on earth was he getting himself involved with here? Should he tell the police? But his father had told him not to, said he'd take a look, and he had to trust what his father said, surely he knew best.

On his way back down a thought struck him. A plan he could put in place that very night. A way he could find out what was happening before Martin got back to him with the translation. If he was right then it would mean that what he was involved in went deeper and darker than he could possibly imagine, and he may well not have enough time before Martin's response reached him.

That night when he went to his room he did not get into bed but instead piled his pillows up in the middle to make it look like he had, and then climbed into the cupboard on the other side of the room, pulling himself into a sitting position amongst the clothes that hung there. The door he kept open just the tiniest bit so that he had a good view across the room, of the bed and more importantly, of the door.

He thought back to dinner. It had been a rather subdued affair. Kerry was still as passive as before, and seemed to be showing no emotions at all, refusing to eat or drink anything, but sitting and staring straight ahead. And what was worse was that Karen had started to look something similar. She was quieter than usual. Sitting still and eating just a tiny portion of the dinner, leftovers from the night before. Nick's father had passed it off as her being worried about Kerry, apparently she had not said more than two words all day.

Nick sat in his hideaway with his eyes glued to the door for a long time and nothing happened. Before too long his eyelids grew heavy and despite how much he tried to fight it, he fell asleep.

He was jolted awake, sometime later, again confused. There was someone in his room. As quietly as possible he moved to get a better view and peered out into the dark room. Karen stood over his bed, she was bending down, reaching with an outstretched arm toward the cover. As she moved lower a ray of moonlight from outside caught a glance across her face and a wave of terror rushed over Nick, he froze again, unable to move. Her face had that same waxen look just like Kerry's, her movements were stiff and clunky, very different to how she normally was, and her eyes were that same strange silver colour. She clasped the end of the duvet and pulled it back, her jerky head movements looking up and down the row of pillows she had not expected to see. He held his breath as she stood tall again, those same jerky movements alien to her usually fluid character, and looked about the room. Slowly she turned and moved across the room toward him, out of view of where he could see. He could not risk opening the door any further for fear of her seeing him, but could hear her movements, and guessing thought she must be to his left, moving along the wall opposite the window.

Inch by careful inch he moved himself round to try and see where she was, his breath still held, unnoticed. She wasn't where he thought she would be. He had lost her. Had she left? He didn't dare to move any further but froze where he was. Where was she?

Suddenly the door flung open and her dead waxen face burst into view. For less than a second they locked eyes. The silver glowed bright in the darkness. Unlike anything he had seen before. The fear ran to the very centre of his being. Her eyes seemed to delve into him, reach deep into the back of his head and scream. It was like her mouth was crying with pain, but if he had looked her mouth was clamped shut, that same expressionless look all over her waxen face.

He tried to scream but nothing came out. His voice was lost. Her eyes seemed to hold him where he was. He couldn't move.

In the next moment she reached out and clasped him

by the arm, dragging him out of the cupboard and onto his feet. Her grip was like ice. She pulled him into the middle of the room and dropped him on the floor, moving round to stand in front of him. As she let go some far-off sense of survival briefly returned and he scrambled backwards aware from her reach, his back hitting the door of the cupboard he had just left. She advanced forward but he sprung again to the left just avoiding her grip. His hand clasped something it came into contact with, it was one of his boots. Without even thinking he swung his arm up and made contact squarely on the side of her head. She fell to one side stunned, but was not knocked over, this bought him precious seconds and he stumbled to his feet and out of the door.

The hallway looked as it always did. Why was it no different? This was no longer real life surely? Without thinking he hurtled down one side of the landing and into his father's room, the master bedroom of the house.

'Dad! Dad,' he screamed, flinging open the door and careering across the uncarpeted floorboards on his bare feet. 'It's Karen, she's...she's.... Dad...?'

His father lay across the sheets of the four-poster bed. He couldn't have been sleeping, his body was cavorting too violently for that. He seemed to be saying something as his torso twisted and turned uncontrollably on the mattress, as if jolts of electricity were being passed through it. Nick leaned in, trying to hear what he was saying.

'What is it dad?' he said.

His father spoke but he couldn't understand him.

'Dad? What is it? Can I help?'

He leaned as close as he could, avoiding his father's flailing limbs and then finally he made something out.

'Karen...' he thought he heard him say. 'Karen! Why? What are you doing Karen?'

Then Karen was in the doorway.

He saw the silver in her eyes before anything else. She stood for a second, an indiscriminate silhouette against an orange glow, and then she jolted forward like the machine she seemed to be.

Instinct took hold once more. Nick threw himself forward and landed at her feet, knocking into her, she toppled over and then losing her centre of gravity continued forwards and collapsed on her side. He didn't stop to look back but continued out of the door. He had to check on Kerry.

She was the same. Still waxen faced but no longer silver eyed. Maybe whatever it was that possessed them could only take them over one at a time? He didn't have any time to think about it though. Kerry's room was a dead end, Karen, or whatever it was that Karen had become, would catch him easily in that tight space. He needed to get upstairs to the attic, where he knew he could lock the door, and where he stood a chance of reading about what the hell might have happened here.

She caught up with him on the landing. Standing the other side of the space and staring with those same glowing silver eyes. Behind her was the staircase to the attic.

Pausing for a second, she moved forward and he slowly circled round the outside, making his way as far round the edge of the large circle landing as he could. She changed her course at the last second and before long was on him again. She was relentless, he just couldn't stop her, her hands grabbing and tearing at him. A stiff fist laid into his back, sending pain splintering through his body, another punch, followed by another caught him in the same spot and winded him. He tried to move forward but she held firm, dragging him by the collar into the middle of the landing whilst he fought for breath. What on earth was she going to do? Before he could find out she made the same mistake and let go of his arm so she could move round to face him. Was she trying to perform some kind of ritual? Winded though he was he didn't need to be told twice and with all his force he swung his legs up to kick her in the face. It felt liking kicking a concrete statue, pain coursing once more through his feet and then into his whole body, but it seemed to work, and she collapsed backwards.

He flipped himself over onto his front and leaped to his feet, he made it a few steps to the bottom of the staircase, and then when trying to take the next step felt his foot caught behind him. Karen was holding onto his leg, slowly pulling herself further forward, that same dulled expression plastered all over her face. Her grip was like iron, she pulled him to the floor once more.

'Just let me go!' he screamed at her, but her expression didn't change.

Now she was at his navel, pulling him down so his back was on the staircase, and her claw like hand pulling harder and firmer at him. With one hand above him clasping the banister he reached slowly forward with the other one, trying first to push her off him before claiming contact with her face. It felt as waxen as it looked. His hands slipped and he could have torn her face from her. She screamed.

A guttural inhuman yell that pierced his very sole.

Her hold loosened. He clawed again at her face, this time getting his nails caught, and the same thing happened. She screamed and forced herself away from him. He looked briefly at his hands. They were covered in what looked like clay. Before she could recover, he was up and to the top of the landing, inside the room with the door locked behind him, his chest heaving with the exertion. After dragging the huge wooden desk so it covered the doorway he looked once more at his hands. Under the dim light of the library it seemed to be red clay that covered his palms and sat under his nails. What the hell did that mean?

Hands shaking he picked up the notebook left discarded on the table. The page was covered in strange symbols accompanied by an explanation in letters he recognised but a language he did not. A translation perhaps, but of what? The symbols seemed vaguely familiar. Next to it lay an open book covered in a thick layer of dust. 'A History of Roman Britain' was open on a page entitled: Aulus Plautius's advance. Apparently in 43BC Aulus Plautius marched his Roman legion from Kent to Colchester and was stopped by the River Thames. He built a bridge over the river, this first 'London Bridge' was thought to be only yards from the present-day London Bridge. So? London Bridge was miles from here. He flung the book back on the table and wandered over to the window. Nothing. Pitch black. Not even the faintest glow of silver he had expected to see rising from the tomb. Why was Karen not trying to get in the room? Was she waiting for him? He yawned and sat by the window, pulling himself up into a tiny alcove and closing his eyes. All he saw when he did was her startling silver ones staring back at him. They were so terrifying, but so captivating at the same time. What did it all mean? He yawned again but knew he wouldn't sleep. This was going to be a long night.

Eventually he plucked up the courage to open the door. The sun had been up for a few hours and the birds were flitting from tree to tree. The day had begun and the world went about its business with no idea what had occurred in number 15 Borderdale Street just hours before.

The coast seemed clear.

Carefully he stepped out of the room, ready to flee back inside should he need to. The stairwell and then the landing were empty. Silence. Not a single sound seemed to occur. He listened hard but there was nothing save the sound of his own feet padding over the floorboards. Gingerly he checked all the bedrooms, but they were empty. Where were they all?

At the bottom of the stairs lay a single envelope beneath the letter box. He picked it up. It was addressed to him. Martin!! He must have translated it. Fast work. If he made it out of this alive, he would really owe him one.

He checked the downstairs rooms but there was still no

sign of anyone. The place as silent as it always seemed to be. Pulling up a chair at the kitchen table he ripped the letter open, barely able to wait any longer, and pulled out the wad of papers inside.

Firstly, there was a handwritten note from Martin:

Nick,

Great to hear from you old chum. How's the new place? Must come up and visit at some point. Everyone from the old gang misses you.

Must say, was pretty shocked to receive your letter. All very strange. You writing a story or something? Where did you find it? Must be some kind of a joke perhaps? Give me a bell when you get this and we can have a chat. In the meantime I've done my best to translate what I can.

Hope to hear from you soon.
Your old pal,
Martin

He opened up the other folded sheets and started to read. He didn't even notice how quickly his heart was beating.

Dear Sir,

If you are reading this letter, then it means I am dead, and you have a great journey ahead of you and an important mission to complete.

My name is Tom Wimpole and I have been living at number 15 Borderdale Street since shortly after I was born. My Great-Grandfather bought this house in the early 1890s, a time when there were few problems or worries for the family, nor the area, and Great Britain was King of its mighty empire.

Then came the Second World War.

It changed everything. Not only for London and Britain but for every family in the country. Perhaps for my own more than most. During the Blitz a bomb landed in the garden and caused the mighty crater that is still evident today.

But it was more than just mud and dirt that was unearthed that fateful day.

It took me forty-eight years but discover the origins of the tomb the bomb uncovered I finally did. It belongs to body of a 14-year-old boy by the name of Timilius.

You must understand this is an area of history that was all but erased as the Romans trudged their unstoppable march across Europe; they took what they wanted and killed those they saw fit and then wrote the history books themselves. Not unlike the Nazis that changed my own fortunes. It is poetic justice that these two great and equally evil empires should bookend the trouble that begat my own life.

Timilus was a member of the Shandalan tribe of Britons that lived in the area that was to become Hackney in about the 1st Century BC. They stood up against Aulus Plautius's legion of Roman soldiers and even managed to destroy the first bridge that they built to cross the Thames, some six miles South of where they lived. You would now know it as London Bridge. The first London Bridge.

In revenge for this they wiped out the entirety of the Shandalan, leaving only Timilus alive, as a warning to the other tribes in the area. The young boy wouldn't take this warning though and stood up to the Romans, fighting and refusing to go quietly. He even managed to wound Plautius himself, a wound that would later kill the general and drive all our fortunes.

As punishment they bound him with leather ties and left him in a stone coffin which they then buried. He was still alive when they placed him in the grave, the stone coffin that to this day remains at the bottom of the garden where they left it some 2,000 years ago.

Along with the history, the inscriptions on the tomb it has taken me some forty years to decipher. It was a form of Gallic spoken by the Britons at the time and whipped out by the Romans with the massacre, written as some kind of sick joke to add insult to extreme injury. A curse that far from killing out the tribe as they so wished has kept its spirit alive longer than the mighty Roman Empire itself lasted.

'Here lies one of the last Britons, imprisoned as a boy forever lain until one of the same age can replace him.' There was a second

section, but I couldn't make out the symbols.

Within weeks of the bomb landing, it was obvious that something had changed. My family moved out after the disappearance of the much-loved family dog and didn't return until the war had finished in 1945. I myself was not born until 1944, away from this house, but I had two older sisters who enjoyed a happy childhood growing up in the house that was once cheery and contented.

When they returned, they saw that London was a much-changed place, but my family couldn't help feeling that nowhere more so than our own once dear house.

My sister fell ill after an elongated period where she became nothing more than a shadow of her former self. She never spoke but stared into thin air for years and years, until finally becoming bed ridden. This was the only way I knew her.

By 1958, when I was 14, the strange goings on intensified. Local animals seemed to be affected by our house, hovering by the perimeter and seeming almost possessed before being dragged away by owners and authorities, and sometimes my own father would...

Here the translation stopped. Apparently there had been some water damage to the last page and Martin had not been able to read any of the words. There were only a few short sections of translation left readable.

...waxen face that is susceptible to human contact and takes on the appearance of the red clay from the earth which it came. Like they had been moulded from the very ground itself.

It's the words. It must be the words. I hadn't spoken them and that is why the curse hasn't been broken. To my eternal damnation when I was filled with the silver spirit I willed it to take my family over me, and it did... I hate myself for it but at least I've been able to work on the translation since. The chance is now yours to put the wrongs committed all that time...

And

Yours with honour,

TW

p.s. Remember the date, 17th February 1958.

Nick looked at the date. It was 17th February 2008. Exactly 50 years since the date given in the postscript. But what did it mean? What words did he need to speak? It must have something to do with the inscription on the tomb. Were those the words he needed to speak on the stroke of fifty years? But how would he know what they were or how on earth to pronounce them. The notebook on the desk in the library! He knew he had seen the symbols before.

He stood from the table and made to leave the room, hardly noticing how his legs were shaking so violently they could barely hold his weight. He needed to get that notebook, it was the key. That must have been the translation that Tom had studied over the last forty odd years. Somehow he had worked out what the inscription said but had died months before being able to speak it. The inscription that needed to be said at the correct time to finally put an end to the curse.

He padded up the stairs again, breathing heavily, only finally aware of how tired he was. He hadn't eaten since dinner the evening before, and hadn't slept a wink. He pressed on, putting the feeling of fatigue behind him. How had Tom survived fifty years earlier when his possessed family had tried to give him to the spirit of Timilius? The curse of the Britons laid on him by the Romans to never rest until he could find someone of the same age he could take the body of. Tom had been 14 then, and Nick was 14 now, he had no intention of letting Timilius take over his body. He had grown fairly attached to it.

At the top of the main staircase he stopped for a second to catch his breathe. What was happening to him? Normally he would be able to push on further than this. He leaned heavily on the banister that ran the width of the large square landing and laid his head on the top of his clasped hand.

Then he heard it.

Soft at first, then increasing in volume until it was obvious. The padding of bare feet on the floorboards. And not just one pair.

Fear surged through him and gave him legs. He leapt forward, toward the short staircase that led back up to the library. He needed to get that book. It was the only way he could think to break the curse. He couldn't be certain, but he had nothing else to go on, if only the rest of the letter hadn't been destroyed, he was sure Tom would have told him exactly what to do.

His legs carried him as far as the bottom of the stair and then they gave way, sending him flailing forward to land with a thumb on the stairs, his head slapped into the hard wood and he saw stars. Forcing himself over onto his back he tried to catch his breath but it seemed so hard. The curse must be affecting him as well. Perhaps this was what happened, the closer it gets to the time, the more power it has, debilitating the subject so they can be carried to the tomb easier and the spirit can enter them.

Nick forced his weary head up and caught a sight that chilled him to the bone. Down the corridor three figures advanced into his view. They walked with that same stilted pace, that inhuman judder that sent a chill of terror coursing through his body. He couldn't move. He was frozen stiff. One by one they filtered into view.

His father led the way, followed by Karen and the Kerry at the back. They walked without breaking stride when they saw him. He twisted over onto his front, seemingly unable to stand, and tried to scramble up the steps to the library. If he was going to stand any chance of stopping the curse he needed to get that notebook. He was forced to his feet and pulled back down to the bottom of the stairs and suddenly his father's face burst into view. His look could not have been more different from how it had been the night before, then he had been twisted over in pain, and now it was as plain faced as the others were. That same waxen look and blinding silver eyes. Nick tried as hard as he could not to look into those eyes. They hauled him back onto the landing and made to drag him down the next set of stairs. A quick look over his shoulder saw the door to the library stood open, beckoning him inside, he wasn't down yet, he needed to break free, get back up there and find that book. He wasn't going to let this curse beat him.

It was then that he remembered old Tom's words...*waxen face that is susceptible to human contact and takes on the appearance of the red clay from the earth which it came.* That hadn't meant much at the time but then he remembered the screams Karen had made the night before and the red clay like substance on his hands. Turning back to face his father he didn't hesitate and slapped him as hard round the face as he could. For a split second nothing happened, everything froze, the shell that was his father stood still and a flicker of confusion seemed to cross over the otherwise lifeless features. With both hands Nick clawed at his face, not letting that strange sensation spreading through his body from the contact overtake him. Soon enough his father's grip loosened and he struggled free, forcing his tired limbs back across the space. Before he could make it far something was on his back, dragging him down to the floor. It was Karen and Kerry, each biting at him with their claw like hands, scratching and tearing at his clothes. He put his hands up to cover his face and with one foot caught little Kerry a glancing blow in the middle of her head. She fell backwards and disappeared from view, an extreme amount of guilt flooding through him at kicking his 18 months old stepsister. Fielding off Karen's blows he told himself over again that it was not her, there was something else occupying her body.

Gaining his composure again he clawed once more at Karen's face, that single piercing scream escaping her mouth once more and stabbing at his ear drums. With all the strength he could muster he pulled himself to his feet and made for the room once more. His father, now recovered, was after him like a shot, but Nick leapt from his reach with just inches between him and his father's outstretched claw like hands. He made it into the room and slammed the heavy oak door behind him. His father's heavy body collided with the door but the old wood held firm. Nick stepped away from the door back into the room, wincing with each new bang on the door. Before long there are three different types of noises on the other side, all three of them must have recovered and were now trying to make their way inside.

His hands were once again shaking as he picked up the small, yellowed notebook on the desk. The corners of the pages turned up showing its age. So this was what was going to save his life then. Sure enough, next to the twisted symbols he recognised from the tomb in the garden were written strange English phrases of the like he had never seen before. He tried speaking the first one, ignoring as best he could the continued thumps on the door.

Wingodiosal Reperartosal Letemnosino Parentasernum Bacer, it said.

'Win-go…o…odi…i…osal…' he repeated as best he could. His voice was broken and empty, almost like it was someone else speaking.

The knocks from outside grew heavier, less disjointed, they were starting to work together.

Taking a deep breath, he tried again.

'Win… Wingodiosal,' he said, finding strength in his success. 'Wingodiosal Reperartosal Letemnosino Parentasernum Bacer!' He near shouted the words out, the last couple feeling like a power was raging through him. At the last moment as the last syllable left his mouth there was a shocking blind of silver light that lasted less than a millisecond but soared through him and toward the door.

The sound of the knocking stopped. Was it the words?

They really did have some power after all. Within the minute though that constant repetitive dull banging was back. So the words had had some affect, they had stopped them, but how? Had they been thrown away, or had they merely stopped because they'd heard them? Either way it meant that there was something there. Perhaps the words had some strength over the spell, but the further away they were from the tomb the less the affect was. He needed to get down there and soon.

Hurtling over to the window he knew instantly this point of exit was his only option. He couldn't fight off the monsters single handily, the adrenaline was starting to fade in his system and that overarching feeling of being drained of all energy had returned. The power from the words had briefly filled him with strength but that too was fading now. The roof was the only option. He flung open the window and thrust his head out into the late morning. It was only 11am but seemed so much later. The sky had a deep covering of thick inky grey clouds from horizon to horizon, the light only just infiltrating to cast a strange kind of half-light not unlike an eclipse across the house and garden. At the end of the roof there was an old oak that sat at the far corner of the house, if he could get along the roof, he stood a chance of climbing onto the branch that met the roof edge and scaling his way down to reach the tomb that way. If he was quick enough there might a chance that his possessed family would still be banging at the library door.

It was high. Too high. Three storeys high and he'd never had much of a head for heights, refusing even to climb into the tree house his old friends back home had built. This was different though and so after taking a deep breath and shoving the notebook in his back pocket he stepped out onto the tiles and inched his way along, the insistent banging from inside spurring him on. The going was tough, but he found himself a rhythm and slowly made his way across the first ten feet without any problems, he found that by not looking down it was much easier to focus and not think of the great height. He tried to focus on a church spire somewhere in the middle distance, he didn't know where it was, for the first time he suddenly realised he had been in this area for several days and no idea what the area looked like, the only time he'd left the house was to go into the back garden. He had become a prisoner.

Whilst his mind wandered a loose tile gave beneath him and he slipped forward, tumbling toward the edge of the roof. His hands grabbed pointlessly at tiles and suddenly he was over the edge, his feet stabbing at nothing but air. A survival instinct from deep inside somewhere kicked in and before he could drop all the way his hands found purchase and clung to the edge of the guttering preventing him from falling at the last moment. He clung there for a few moments, his body flailing around in mid-air with no idea what to do. He tried haling himself up but couldn't find the strength. Worse than that the notebook from his back pocket had slipped out and was gone. How was he going to speak the words now?

Looking over to his right the tree was not that far away. Perhaps he could reach it by swinging himself over. Slowly but surely he built up the momentum and then shimmied himself across a few holds before stopping again, he could reach the tree with his foot. Taking a deep breath he moved a few more handle holds and found himself a couple of feet nearer. Before long he could reach out with one hand and touch the outstretched branch, which seemed to lean back at him as if trying to take his hand. He moved a couple more spaces and then found some footing on one of these outstretched branches, after a few more steps he let the branch take his weight and then a couple more and he had let go of the roof completely. He breathed a sigh of relief and took a few more steps, hugging the trunk of the tree and squatting down to take a look below. No sign of the notebook. What was he going to do? Could he remember the words?

Before he could think the branch he had his footing on started to sag. It wasn't going to hold his weight for much longer. He stumbled onto the next one down and shifted his weight forward, moving as quickly as he could from one to the other. When he was some ten feet off the ground he misjudged the thickness of a branch he stood on and it snapped, sending him sprawling forward into the air. For a brief moment he was weightless. Free falling forward those ten feet to land with a thump on his back. Everything went black.

The next thing he could remember was a feeling of weightlessness. As if he was being transported a few feet above the ground. Floating through the garden.

Where was he? What had he been doing?

None of it seemed to make sense, no memories would return. The feeling wasn't an unpleasant one though, if he relaxed perhaps everything would be ok.

His eyes blinked open. There was a face floating above him. He knew that face. There was a memory there somewhere, deep inside the recesses of his mind. Who was it? Someone he knew very well. He blinked again and his eyes flickered open to reveal more of the figure. It was his father. But he looked different. His expression was blank and lifeless. It was like his face was made of wax. Slowly, piece by piece, the world came back into focus. He wasn't floating at all. He was being carried. His father was carrying him.

Then it all came back.

He struggled to free himself but was held hard in the hands of his captures. They were in the garden, heading back down the slope he had fallen down those few days before. They were taking him to the tomb, he was going to be sacrificed to bring back the ancient Briton boy.

He tried to scream but his voice was muffled by something. No words came out. The words! What were the words? If he could only remember them and speak them at the right time, he could end all of this and free his family from the curse. What were they? He tried to focus but the fall made it hard. His head kept spinning and a surge of pain splintered down his back with every step. The shock was wearing off and the pain was taking over. What were those words?!!

'Win… Wingodiosal,' he said, and there was the slightest hint of a pause in his father's advance. That was it! That was the first word. Once again spurred on by his success he repeated it, louder this time, and there was another more obvious pause in his father's movement.

'Wingodiosal Reperartosal…' he said and there was a flinch in the hold. It was looser. With all the strength he could muster he jolted himself forward and sent his own body spinning toward the ground. He landed with a thump and as disorientated as he was, he somehow pulled himself to his feet and found himself running. The tomb burst into his vision. It was glowing silver. There couldn't be much time left.

'Wingodiosal Reperartosal…' he repeated over and over again, unable to remember the last few words, each time he did the tomb seemed to glow slightly more and then fade again to a constant dull silver. Swinging round the three former members of his family stood in a small clearing in the undergrowth, keeping their distance from him. It must be the words, they were keeping them back.

'Lete… lete…' he started, but just couldn't remember the third word. Above him mighty clouds swirled as thunder and lightning began to crash and rain down upon the scene. He couldn't be sure if it was everywhere or just this garden, but at that moment there was nowhere else, the garden and the house were everything to him and he knew he must speak those words, or they would be everything to everyone.

And then they came to him. All the words in one go. It was as if he had been filled with a spirit that took him over

much like the possessed family stood before him. He knew
it all. He knew Tom Wimpole, what he looked like, the
feelings he had had and the horrors he felt. He knew who
Timilius was and all about the Tribe and most of all he saw
Aulus Plautius. He saw him right in front of him. He stood
tall, taller than Nick's father, clad in bright white body
armour and glowing silver. He pointed his sword straight
at Nick and as he opened his mouth to speak Nick found
he also had the words, he spoke them along with him.

'Wingodiosal Reperartosal Letemnosino Parentasernum
Bacer,' he said, his voice nothing more than a whisper.
Was it his voice that said it? Was it not Aulus Plautius?
Where had he gone? The vision had vanished. It hadn't felt
like he had said the words at all but something had spoken
through him. He looked down at his hands. They were
paler, not waxen as he had feared but different none the
less. He felt strange. Not weak again but full of something,
like he was being filled with power or strength, like a spirit
was slowly filling him up.

He glanced over at his family; the spell seemed to have
been broken. They no longer appeared to be possessed but
were starting at each other with confusion and fear
covering their features, clearly with no memory of what
had happened. Karen picked up Kerry, who had started to
cry. His father comforted them both and then looked up at
Nick, only then catching sight of him. He moved forward
a few yards and Nick breathed a sigh of relief, it was over,
he had done it, he had saved his family and broken the
spell. He reached out his arm toward his father, but the old
man cringed away.

'Who are?!' he said, fear cracking his voice.

'Dad? It's me,' replied Nick, unsure what was going on.
He made to step forward, but he flinched back away,
standing in front of Karen and Kerry who stared up at him
with wide eyes and fear filled expressions. What had
happened to him?

'What have you done to my family? Where is my son?

What have you done to us!?' his father screamed, holding himself up to his full height, Nick could still see the terror on his face, it was the first time he had seen his father like this.

He looked again at his hands. They didn't seem any different. Why were his family so scared? Stumbling back a step he hit the tomb behind him and swung himself round, an idea growing inside his mind. It was that same dull silver glow. He reached out and without much difficulty lifted the lid off the top. Had it been that light before? It was empty. Where had the body of the boy gone? Slowly his vision started to blur. A flash of silver caught behind his eyes and pressed hard on his brain like a particularly bad headache. He screamed in anguish as the throbbing grew and grew until he it was like a spear was being driven through his head. He felt himself being dragged down to the ground. He was covered in leather straps. They seemed to grow from the ground and tighten themselves around him, dragging him further down and down, forcing him down to his knees, until he was lying on his side. He looked up at the tomb and saw for the first time what was written there. They were words he could understand, words he could read. Had they been there before? No. These were not written in English, it was the same spiralled symbol writing that had been there before, but now he could read it.

It said:

'Here lies one of the last Britons, imprisoned as a boy forever lain until one of the same age can replace him. Speak the words to release the curse and take on the burden of being him…'

The last thing Nick remembered as his conscious self was falling back onto his side as he was dragged by the leather binds into the heart of the tomb. He saw the family of three no longer waxen but teary faced standing by the side, looking down, any sense of fear or terror replaced by confusion as they saw him retreat into the dulled silver tomb.

'Nick…?' he thought he heard his father say, but could have been wrong…

THE END

www.ingramcontent.com/pod-product-compliance
Lightning Source LLC
Chambersburg PA
CBHW050943050726
47592CB00007B/2416